She Was Only Mine

SHE WAS ONLY MINE

ABHINAV OJHA

BLOOMSBURY
NEW DELHI · LONDON · OXFORD · NEW YORK · SYDNEY

BLOOMSBURY INDIA
Bloomsbury Publishing India Pvt. Ltd
Second Floor, LSC Building No. 4, DDA Complex, Pocket C – 6 & 7,
Vasant Kunj, New Delhi, 110070

BLOOMSBURY, BLOOMSBURY INDIA and the Diana logo
are trademarks of Bloomsbury Publishing Plc

First published in India 2025

Copyright © Abhinav Ojha, 2025

Abhinav Ojha has asserted his moral rights to be identified as the author of
this work in accordance with the Indian Copyright Act, 1957

This is a work of fiction. Unless otherwise indicated, all the names,
characters, businesses, places, events and incidents in this book are either
the product of the author's imagination or used in a fictitious manner.
Any resemblance to actual persons, living or dead, or actual events is
purely coincidental

All rights reserved. No part of this publication may be: i) reproduced or
transmitted in any form, electronic or mechanical, including photocopying,
recording or by means of any information storage or retrieval system
without prior permission in writing from the publishers; or ii) used
or reproduced in any way for the training, development or operation
of artificial intelligence (AI) technologies, including generative AI
technologies. The rights holders expressly reserve this publication from
the text and data mining exception as per Article 4(3) of the Digital Single
Market Directive (EU) 2019/790

ISBN: 978-93-69524-72-3
2 4 6 8 10 9 7 5 3 1

Typeset in Minion Pro by Manipal Technologies Limited
Printed and bound in India by Gopsons Papers Pvt. Ltd., Noida

To find out more about our authors and books visit www.bloomsbury.com
and sign up for our newsletters

Dedicated to Mr. Aarav Tripathi.
Thanks for allowing me to make modifications to your story.

1

March 2021, Patna

'I had no wounds, but I was bleeding'. Life had taken a full circle. I was looking at myself in the same mirror which I was staring into with my hairstyle back when I was going to Delhi for my first-ever corporate job in HCL. I still remember how excited I was about my job and how I styled my hair and looked more than a dozen times in the mirror. I was in love with seeing my face and staring at the mirror, but it was not the case anymore.

I was a coward, I could see a selfish human-being in me. I was not bothered about my hairstyle or how I looked. All that excitement had dissipated. I had no idea what was next inline for me. *I have always believed in destiny, but I hate mine.* After letting my emotions flow through my teary, red eyes, all I wanted was to lock myself in my room and let the emotional storm inside me burst out. I had lost my appetite and had no food for the last two days. Even a full glass of water was not possible to consume because of my sore throat. I had stopped working for my job, and I had received several warnings of termination.

I love Swati but what should I do now, if I ever meet her, what should I tell her that I am a loser, I lost the most important bet of my life, how will I be able to look into her eyes? Am I dumping her? Plenty of questions were hovering like bees around my mind, and that stung. After thinking about all this for a while, I decided to put curtains on the mirror I used to love and denied myself seeing my face. I was a cheater, and I wasn't good enough to see myself anymore.

It was around 11 PM and I had to do the most strenuous task of my life. I had to remove Swati from my life. I knew that I could not remove her from my heart, as she had already won it with her love and care. I sat on my bed and drank a small glass of water. I took my phone with my shaking hands and decided to remove photos of her. It was getting hard to breathe, I was coughing and shivering. The more I was deleting her photos, I was trembling. It with my emotional pain that was teetering me, I sensed I was going far away from Swati with every deleted photos.

My soft heart did not allow me to delete any more memories of her. I brought my phone towards my lips and I kissed Swati's photo on the screen and gained some more strength to delete more. I deleted all our memories and her pics from my phone. I don't know what would she think of me, she would be eagerly waiting for me in Delhi. I wept for her, but it was my soul that broke that day. *I was in such emotional pain that even if I had died that day, my soul would not agonize and beg for its survival.* Even after deleting Swati's memories from everywhere, she was still there in my eyes, in my dreams, waiting for me to return and take care of her. '*I did not know who writes destiny, whoever has written mine might have special enmity against me*'.

After deleting all of our memories, my heart was ripped apart and shattered into pieces. I was coughing incessantly, and I blocked Swati from my contacts and social media accounts and broke my sim card. I had no courage to see and go through our past chatting text, and I closed my eyes while deleting our entire chat history. *I used to hear how people endure pain while dying, but there is a heaven that welcomes them after their death. Here I was dying and still breathing, and there was hell waiting to worship my entire life.*

After going through all my mental toughness and struggle, I felt like my soul left my body, I had no emotions left, I was alive, but I was not. I didn't know whether I would be able to see my love for one last time. I don't know what Swati will go through after knowing all this that has happened. There were plenty of unanswered questions bubbling in my mind. It was a very long night for me, the longest that I ever had in my life. All that I did was to shed tears in love for Swati. She had made me who I was today, and it felt like everything was lost. I was going through every single thing that I feared.

After tossing and turning for more than a hundred times that night, I was still remembering all our past trips and all the memories that we had. Her smile was twinkling in my eyes and I could hear her calling me '*Aye Tripathi*', when are you coming back. She was in love with me, and she trusted me that I would take care of her. She would not forgive herself for loving a cheater and a selfish human-being like me. She was a girl full of love and life, and I didn't know how she would handle this situation.

After not having any food for almost 5 days and locking myself inside my room without having any sort of communication with my family members. I decided to leave my house not because I was going to join a new job, but to spend time alone and hate myself for what I had done. I would move to any unknown place far away from any people that were closer to me and let my emotions burst out. I was struggling to handle my emotions and tears in front of my family members. I wanted God to curse me for whatever I have done with Swati and give her all my happiness for her life.

I lied to my family and told them that I have joined a new job in Kolkata ….. I left for Kolkata within a day …

3 Years Back

2

April 2018, Patna

'Mr. Aarav Tripathi, get ready quickly, you are getting late for the train" my mom shouted. I sprinted and looked in the mirror, and I had a habit of glancing at my mirror more than 100 times in a day. I thought I looked good enough to attract anyone. While gazing at myself in the mirror, I flashed back to my early teenage days when I was studying in my primary school and my mother used to comb my hair every day and I would get teased by my school classmates deeming it a 'chipku' hairstyle. When I was in secondary school and when I studied in engineering college in Dhanbad, I paid specific attention to how my hair looked. I do not let anyone touch my hair.

It was around 8 PM, and I was to board the Rajdhani express, which arrived at Patna Junction at 21:30. It would reach me in New Delhi at around 10AM in the morning. I should reach the Station by 9:15, I thought to myself. I was rummaging around my room and getting my bag ready to leave for my first ever corporate job. After graduating from the Birsa Institute of Technology(BIT), Sindri, Dhanbad, from Computer Science and Engineering (CSE). I was placed at HCL with a 10 lakhs per annum package. I was getting a little late, I rushed to my mom and asked her to make me an 'adrak wali chai'. Trust me, my mom is the worst chai maker ever, and she has no regrets at all.

I belong to a middle-class brahmin family of five people. My Grandfather is a retired government school principal and also the Principle of our house whose nickname is the "Pension man". My grandmother has no work to do; hence she is the cashier of the house. My father is a current bank employee in SBI and is the HOD of our House. Without his consent, no one can work. My mother is the lecturer. The only common thing between all of us was our unfathomable love and adoration for tea, and we all live together in our Home Sweet Home with lots of love between us in Exhibition Road, Patna.

Get ready Aarav, your show off days are gone now, work hard and build your career, my mom threw a taunt at me while I was looking around the mirror a couple of times.

I already had plenty of lectures in my engineering college mom, it's time to luxuriate in my life and have some good fun, I countered her.

Don't argue, she raised her voice.

Where is my special 'adrak chai' mom? You're getting me late now. I pleaded her to hand over my tea as soon as possible.

After a few minutes, My mom came hurrying in and gave me a cup of tea, which I sipped right away and also spit it because of the bad taste, there was no taste of sugar in the tea.

Is this a good tea mom, how can someone be so bad at making chai even after so many years of cooking experience, I complained to her and expressed my dissatisfaction.

Same as you engineers do nothing and hustle around for higher package even after so many years of working experience, she giggled sarcastically.

I am getting late mom and you are cracking jokes. Don't bring In engineers everywhere, you already know that I am placed at an impressive package in a top MNC, I retaliated to her sarcasm.

I will not bring in engineers, please bring in your wife so that she can cook well and make you good chai, she responded to me with a very unflattering tone.

That's fine mom, you won't make yourself better at making tea, but you want me to get married to someone who can cook good food and chai, that's all you need Right? I asked my mom.

Yes, that's all I need. Get married and ask her to make you a good chai. I'm not getting younger to satisfy all your wishes. Now get ready and double-check for all your important files and accessories, she prodded me with her rasping voice.

And what if she is good at cooking and can also make good chai, and you become jealous and insecure about her? What's your guarantee, mom? I quizzed my mom with a sarcastic remark with a grin on my face.

She did not utter a word in response but signaled me to pack my bags.

I checked my pocket for my mobile phone, I intensively double-checked my bag for my charger, my power bank, my wallet, and my credit and debit cards, my laptop, and it's charger and all my important files and documents before showing thumps up to my mom.

It was around 8:30, and I frantically made my way out of my room with my bag to the main hall where my father, along with my grandparents, were having some interesting conversation. Time was slipping away quickly, and I was running late for my train. I immediately touched the feet of my grandparents, my father and my furious mother, and I was about to head out my 'home sweet home'.

Take these notes beta, you modern-day guys don't keep cash in your hands, my grandfather stood up from his Principles chair and gave me some cash, it was 2000 rupees with a mix of 100 and 200 notes. There is a tradition in my family that whenever someone leaves the house, they are handed over with some cash in their hands. It expresses love and deep affection for each other. It's mandatory, no matter how much you earn. I kept the cash given by my grandfather straight away in my wallet and stuffed it inside my back pocket.

My father never gives me any cash before I leave, but he makes sure I keep all of my notes in a safe place. He shares with me an example of how he handles cash in his bank. I am really proud of my father, I mused to myself.

Keep some of your notes inside the bag you're carrying rather than in the wallet, my father instructed.

Why papa? I asked.

What if your wallet gets stolen, you will not be left with any money or your credit-debit cards, and you will run into a problem, it's better to have some of your cash stashed inside your bag rather than keeping it all in your wallet.

Being a well-versed engineer, I found this training pretty helpful. Although I knew I would still have my Phone to pay via UPI if my wallet gets stolen, but what if my phone also gets stolen, I thought to myself. I immediately kept some cash in one of my trouser pockets inside my bag, and my father gave me a satisfaction-filled smile.

It was 8:45 PM, and I was about to head out of my house, my father used to always ride me to the railway station on his bike even when I was studying in my engineering college. He is following the same protocol even now. He brought his high mileage ancient bike, which I have never ridden in my life since I feel it's not a bike but an enhanced version of a cycle.

Please change the bike papa, you don't have to spend anything now on my education, I will earn for my living, please get a decent bike please, I begrudgingly asked and made a request.

Good people don't ride sports bikes like you, we are decently working people, I will have a new bike but only Hero or Honda and nothing else, said my father a bit reluctantly.

Having an argument with my father is same as writing an engineering mathematics paper in engineering semesters, you will certainly not pass in the first attempt. I gave up straight away and said, as you wish, papa.

My father throttled out his bike with so much pride, and it made a very annoying noise, he shifted the gear to neutral and demonstrated to me his bike engine sound by taking the long accelerator with a very devious smile. I had understood what he was specifically trying to say. I touched the feet of my mother and grandparents for the final time, and sat on the most luxurious bike I could ever sit.

I raised my left hand and waved to all my wonderful people, my family, and I was just about to leave to the Patna railway station for my train. My father changed the gear to No 2 and then 3 and we moved forward.

3

I have 20 years of experience, you fool, don't try to teach me how to ride a bike, my father lashed out at me furiously when I encouraged him to drive faster. He switched to gear no 3 on his super old bike and was riding the bike at 30 km/hour on an uncrowded road. I adjusted my ass on the rigid back seat of the luxuriant bike. Whenever he tried to accelerate the bike, it did not go past 40 km/hour, I was intently looking at the speed meter of the bike constantly and that irritated me. Because of excessively slow riding in the past, the bike engine had already given up his desires to run at a full top speed. I heard the bike saying' apun slow hee daurega'. Meanwhile, my father was describing to me the countless advantages of using his bike, such as its light weight, excellent mileage, decent appearance, and affordability. When I tried to impart some knowledge and information about sports bikes to him, he insulted me by saying that a 'sports bike is a nude bike', you can't make someone like your mother sit on the back seat of a sports bike. I was good at engineering mechanics, but I had no answers to my fathers 'nude bike' verdict. I just gave up on winning the argument, same as I had given up on permutations and combinations in Engineering Mathematics without any ray of hope.

He kept on giving me suggestions such as don't drink, don't get close to girls, don't make dozens of friends, do whatever you are supposed to do, build and hone your career and make your father proud. I wanted to react to all his suggestions, but that sluggishness riding on the bike had already irked me more than my engineering lectures listening from a boring professor.

He took the brake and slowed down the bike at a temple. We always adhered to a tradition of going to that temple before we move out of our house for any work or while we were travelling. It's necessary to take the blessings of the Maa Durga temple. We got down from the bike, offered our prayers, took blessings, prasad and tika and continued our slow riding.

It was around 9:00 PM, and we were anxiously rushing to the Patna railway station. My ticket was already booked in 2nd AC, so there was still a half an hour left for the train to arrive at the station. I preferred to book ticket in second AC most of the time mainly because I was one of those who found it too arduous to fall asleep on a railway berth and the purpose of booking a second AC ticket was simply because the coach provides the curtains which I can slide in and none would see me glaring at my mobile screen for entire night. I was a shrewd guy.

Having half an hour in my hands, I had the perfect opportunity to have a cup of tea at the station, since I did not have that back home when I was given a flavorless chai by my mom.' Can we have a cup of tea papa? I requested my father, to which he agreed.

However, my whole Tripathi family is a tea lover; whenever my dad enters my house from any direction, he asks my mother to make chai. Each time she makes chai, either for family members or guests, it's like a necessity for her to take a sip from that chai. If she makes chai 10 times a day, she will drink it every one of the time just for taste. I frequently fight with my mom for making the worst chai ever. I had a terrible argument with her the day when one of the guests refused to drink my mother's hand-made chai while making a very bizarre face. It dented my ego and I advised my mom to take training classes for making good chai.

The train was to arrive in next 15 minutes and I and my dad were having a thoughtful discussion on studies and career. My dad was a perfectionist and a teacher before he got the job at a government bank, so I should always tilt my head and listen to what he's saying. He is the HOD of our house. You can't even buy an item for you without his consent, even when you are paying the money for it. Everyone listens to our HOD. More than having a chai sip, he inquired solely about my most important papers and files, which I should triple-check before leaving. I reconfirmed my job offer files, documents, mark sheets in my bag before we paid the shopkeeper and sprinted towards the railway platform. The train was to arrive now at platform no 1, and it was announced on the speaker. Just a few minutes Before the train arrived my father said, settle well, earn good so that I can get you married to a good girl. 'zamana kharab hai' he further added.

He was not aware about the conversation I had with my mom back home, I was supposed to get married to a girl only if she makes good food and chai, I was tempted to respond, but I chose to remain silent and donned a good beaming smile.

The train has arrived at the platform beta, he indicated in a soft tone. I know how much my father loved me. He was the first one to burst into tears when I left my home for my engineering studies. I looked up my ticket No, which was B2,9 and fastened my legs to get into the B2 coach.

I got inside the coach and sat on my lower berth. Since I struggle to sleep on train berth, I always opt for lower berth when reserving my ticket. I sat down and put aside my bag on the berth, opened my shoes and looked at my father who was still waiting on the platform, glancing from the window outside. He was strolling near to my coach on the railway platform.

It was around 9:45 PM and I heard the loud clanging sound and the train started accelerating slowly. My father strolled with the train coach alongside me following the train's slow pace and waved at me. I waved him back and the train began to accelerate at a full speed. I soothed myself and plopped down on my train berth, dreaming about my first day of my first-ever corporate job in HCL.

4

Go straight forward and turn right, you will find the exit gate, the RPF constable directed. Because I had never been to Delhi before, I was unfamiliar with the platform. I had arrived here just a few moments ago and was floundering around on the platform. I stepped out of the exit gate as instructed by the constable and quickly picked up my phone to inform my mom that I had safely reached New Delhi. My HCl office was located in Sector 126 Noida, which was almost 20 km away from the railway station.

I had some biscuits and tea at the railway outskirts, and I looked through my bag again for all the important documents. After reaching Delhi, I faced the most daunting task of finding a PG in sector 126 in close vicinity to my HCL office, inside a distance of 2–3 kilometers. I reached out to a few PG owners since I was recommended by all my senior working friends to leave in a PG initially, work in the company, get a few new friends and then get a flat where all of them can stay together. I deemed that advice very valuable. After getting in touch with so many PG owners, I stumbled upon SOHA PG which was located in Raipur Khadar, Sector 126, Noida to be a suitable fit for me since it had single rooms available, and it was just 1 km walking distance to HCL, sector 126 campus, and I was the sort of person who was not at all comfortable staying with others in the same room and the reason for that was I used to stay haphazardly and filthy, I did not have any concerns about anything present in the room. I had a fierce argument with one of my roommates a long before when I was in the first year of my engineering college, and from then I have always preferred to remain in a single room. When I searched for the sector 126 area on Google,

I found that it was a highly developed area with a mix of commercial, educational, and IT-related uses. It's close to the express highway and an airport, and there are excellent public transportation options available. The area has many educational institutions, such as Amity University, Mayur School, and Lotus Valley School. Sector 126 is home to several big IT companies, such as HCL, Samsung, and Mahindra, as well as Kotak Bank. The rent for the PG was, 15000 per month for single sharing, which was a reasonable price for me since it also included the cost of food. Initially, my plan was to stay in a PG for only a month or two. I swirled my eyes around to see if there were any taxis. Eventually, I decided to book an Ola. I booked it through the App and the cab was to arrive in the next 20 minutes, and I took the opportunity to have a 360-degree view of the entire railway station. I was overwhelmed and anxious at the same time. It was my first job, and now I would be earning my salary. I worked extremely hard to get a decent package, I tried to energize myself.

The cab arrived, and I got in, gave the OTP for verification, and we were good to go. The driver was munching some *'paan'* in his mouth and he could barely speak. I took the front seat, and he gestured me to tie the seat belt without uttering a word.

How long will it take to get there, bhaiya? I asked the driver with an ebullient tone.

He tentatively attempted to speak with his partially open mouth but pulled himself back after an effort and pointed out me his index finger indicating 1 hour.

Okay, I understood and choose to remain quiet.

After 15 minutes of driving, I noticed that the driver had taken out a tiny dust bin that was placed beneath his seat itself. He threw the *paan* inside that tiny dustbin and pushed the dustbin back, drank a cup of water, and flashed me a warm smile revealing his life-threatening red teeth.

I pondered whether I should ask him for some more detailed information about the small dustbin simply because the dustbin looked like a good invention, but my inner self did not allow, and I passed a beaming smile.

While I was so drowsy and slumbering, the driver interrupted. Are you new to this city? He asked, chewing pan masala.

I said yes, I am new, I got placed in HCL, and I am joining my first ever corporate job from Monday. I responded to him cheerfully with pride.

He inquired, "Do you need any flats?"

I already knew that people around engineering colleges or corporate areas also work as brokering agents and charge the broker's fee or commission to get some new people in the room or flat. I had already communicated with Soha PG directly through Google Business and I said, I have decided to remain in PG as of now instead of flats.

He did not utter a word, there was no opportunity for any sort of financial gains from me.

Well, everything was going as planned when I found that the driver was a notorious guy. He played some Bhojpuri songs at full volume and was intently staring at all the girls who were moving by through the window. Although I have been fond of Bhojpuri songs since I was a Bihari, but did not like the idea of gawking at girls. I felt so awkward, and I was not showing my face towards the driver.

After driving for a while, we got stranded in traffic. The cab driver was someone who could not remain silent for even a few seconds. He was talkative. I tried to avoid him and pulled out my phone and began to read some romantic love stories e-books to distract my mind.

Are you busy somewhere? He interrupted again while peeking into my phone.

Yes, I was reading a book, I responded with a fake smile.

Do you love books? He inquired.

Yes, I am very passionate about books and would also like to write a romantic book if I had the time. I got intrigued by his question since there was some positive conversation going on regarding books and I had a great love for love stories since my younger days.

Even I like romantic books, he responded back.

Do you really? What genres of romance have you read and by which author? I asked out of sheer curiosity with an exuberant smile on my face.

When I was very young, I used to read "manohar kahaniya", he responded as he turned his face towards me.

Are you talking about adult love stories? I shot back.

No, no, it's romantic, he responded with certainty.

He was referring to adult stories as romantic stories. He was obviously around 27–28 years of age and I could not figure out what young age he was talking about, and he used to read adult love stories probably at 16-17. I thought to myself. This person seemed very alarming to me.

Who said you those are romantic stories? I poked him again.

Romance is love and these are love making stories, he responded with a bright smile.

There is no point of having further discussions with him. I thought to myself and decided to keep my mouth closed until I reached the Soha PG. I plugged my earphones and started humming to my songs to avoid him.

I only desired to reach Soha PG as early as possible. Just 4 KMS left to reach Soha Pg. The driver got frustrated, probably without having any single word or conversation with me in the past 20 minutes, and he dialed one of his friends to arrange wine for him when he would return to his home at around 9 PM. I honestly did not like how he behaved.

After dealing with him for an entire one hour, I eventually reached the Soha PG. I got down from the Ola cab, took my bags and paid the amount. I rushed towards the PG office, which was located on the ground floor of the 4-storey building.

5

"Please come inside", the bearded office guy gestured. I stepped into the office. He graciously provided me with a glass of water and a chair to have a seat on. I was lethargic and drowsy, so I instantly drank that cold water like a crow and quenched my thirst and sat down on the chair. I took a long sigh of relief, rested and dropped my bag on the near-by table and was impatiently waiting for the real person to arrive that owns the Soha PG.

Please wait, sir is arriving in a few minutes, the office guy made a request.

Sure no worries, I nodded

After 15 minutes, the owner of the PG, Mr. Kalpesh, arrived. He himself introduced his name to me. I stood up in respect as I belong to a well-educated family and I knew how to show respect for elders. I apparently did this to have a good first impression of mine on him.

Please take your seat, he gestured out with his hands and took a vacant chair to have a conversation with me.

He was a tall man with less hair on his head, probably around 5 feet 10 inches. But the most unpleasant part was that he was, too, chewing on some sort of thing. I sharpened my eyes and tried to figure it out, it would be some sort of gutka. I have heard that people who have less hair on their heads are actually very wealthy and running PG was the real business which didn't need any effort and was all profit. He grew a very dark, rounded mustache to show his quality of manliness, however his extremely high high-pitched sharp voice indicated something else. I wondered PG name is Soha, but the owner's name is Kalpesh, which I investigated and found out that the owner's daughter's name is Soha. Trust me, I had no desire to look at his daughter, no matter if she was beautiful, hot or not. Nevertheless, I did not like the name Kalpesh, my inner self was nicknaming it as 'Kalesh'. I was thinking to myself, what if this PG owner happens to turn out to be a kalesh guy. But, I was frazzled and worn-out, I was not in a mood to mess around in the heat and search for different PG's. I would go with compromise and settle down to any PG. My only criteria was that the PG should be a secure place to live in without any hindrances.

What's the monthly rent, uncle, I was curious just to compare it with the online rent and the original rent.

Single, double, or triple, he responded with his puckered mouth.

I understood that he was asking for single sharing, double or triple sharing. Single sharing uncle, as I had previously discussed on the call, I reminded him.

Rs, 15000 per month for single, 10000 for double and 7000 for triple, he replied.

Fooding included, he further added, but was unclear because of his constant chewing.

I heard it as fooling included, I got nervous. Am I at the right place, I asked myself? I wiggled my eyes and stared back and forth.

He understood from my body language that I was mumbling about something. Fooding is also included in this amount, he clarified in a strong tone.

I nodded.

I never liked anyone who stayed in the same room along with me because I was the world's sloppiest guy. I don't bother trying to keep my surroundings clean, which had always led to problems with my roommates in the past. I was still appeased by the PG, since it was just a make shift PG for me, I wasn't going to stay there for long. I was planning to make new friends and move in to a new flat … Anyway, I had a doubt regarding the quality of the food that was served in the PG.

How's the food, uncle? Are there cooks in the PG? I quizzed him.

Yes, we have 4 cooks along with supporting workers who cook food every day in the cooking area, the food is good and no one has ever had a complaint until now, he exaggerated about the positive elements of his PG.

I was very fatigued. Everything was cleared, and I was asked to make one month's advanced payment along with the running month payment as rent. I straight away took out my brand new IPhone X and displayed my Apple logo to the uncle. I was like uncle, 'I am not poor. You should be treating me with respect.' I scanned the QR code and made the money transfer through UPI, and Mr. Kalpesh called for his office guy to show me the room.

Oh, Aarav! You are such a dumb guy, you paid two months of advanced payment, and you have not even seen the room. What foolish thing have you done, I thought to myself. What if, the rooms are not good enough. I was tensed and scared, I remembered seeing the rooms on Google Business profile before reaching here, but that does not necessarily mean that those rooms were real.

I walked sluggishly through the stairs and reached the 2nd floor as instructed by the office guy. I entered the room and moved my eyes to every corner. There was a long bed and a big open window in one corner. There were tables and chairs provided beside the bed for working. There was a common washing machine too for each floor; However, the attached bathroom was tiny. I did not like it. On the whole, the PG was like 50 to 50 for me.

Did you like the room? The office guy asked graciously.

It is good, I faltered and donned a fake smile.

Alright then, you can shift now and take some time to get some rest. When is your office joining date? He further asked.

It's from Monday, I responded tirelessly.

He was a pleasant guy, and he made sure that I was comfortable. I locked the room from inside, drank some water and settled my bag on the bed. I spread up my bedsheet and air pillow on the bed and relaxed my body for a few minutes before I went to use the teeny tiny bathroom for a cold nude bath.

6

"I will be late mom" I pleaded with my over proud mom to disconnect the call. It was close to 9 AM, and I was running late for the first day of my office. I meticulously dressed in a formal white shirt and black pants, ensuring that my black leather shoes were sparkling black. Additionally, I donned a classy golden color wristwatch to enhance my looks, and a rectangular modern pair of glasses to show off my personality. I drizzled a bit of a perfume, and I was almost ready to leave. I reached for my bag and checked it for the hard copy of documents I was supposed to submit to the onboarding team. I was carrying the joining letter in my hands, and I was all eager to step out of Soha PG.

The office was not more than 1 km from my PG, I could have walked, but I still decided to take a cab because it was scorching hot outside, and I did certainly not wish to go to the office filthy and dripping with sweat. I firmly believed in the first impression is the last impression concept. I took a cab and headed to my office.

It only took me around 5 minutes to reach the Gate 3 of HCL campus, which was located at Technology Hub, SEZ, Plot Number-3A, Near Lotus Valley, Noida Sector 126. Immediately upon stepping onto the campus, I was in a state of awe when I saw the majestic beauty of the campus. I widened my eyes to each corner of the enormous HCL building. The campus, spread over a plot of 54 acres and total built-up area of 4.35 million square feet, was planned in phases. The campus consists of corporate block, software blocks, BPO blocks, infrastructure block, cafeterias and a medical center including sports facilities and water bodies. There were six towers and 3 cafeterias altogether. There were three entrance Gates. Looking at the stupendous infrastructure of the campus, I got extremely proud of myself, and I was excited about the opportunity to work in HCL as a software engineer.

It was shortly after 10 AM, and I was asked to move to Tower 3 and all of us, including me and other freshers who were impatiently waiting outside, went inside Tower 3 straight into the waiting hall which was located on the ground floor of the Tower 3. In about 15 minutes from then, a member of the onboarding team dressed entirely in black suit and pants came hurrying in and beckoned us to head to the meeting room which was there at the ground floor only at a minimal distance.

We proceeded to the meeting room with great pride and joy. Almost all the freshers were extremely jovial. I rolled my eyes to see if there were any girls where I can sit beside them in the meeting room and have a small chat with them. I observed that most of the girls freshers among 100 freshers were clustered in the first two rows of the meeting room. I spotted out some empty seats and rushed to take the seat only to watch that some naughty mannerless freshers were sprinting like a dog to sit there. I got disappointed and began to look for other seats. I figured out an empty seat between two guys in the third row, but I had no other choice but to go there and sit. I seated myself and rested my body, picked my bag and cradled it in my lap, and chugged some water from my bottle. After listening to a few words from both the boys sitting left and right towards me, I found two distinctly different characters. Left to me was Rohan, who was very talkative and friendly and naughty too. Right to me was Kreepesh, who was very silent and focussed only on his career. And in the middle was Me, who had the characteristics of both the characters, a friendly naughty guy who was focused on his career. It was a few hours of fun chatting with both of them.

Beginning your career as a fresher in HCL was a dream job for so many, There were altogether 100 freshers who were asked to report that day. We were told to submit all our hard copies of our important files, which were mark sheets of our college, passing certificate of college, address proof and other required documents. Upon verification of the documents by the onboarding team, An induction program was scheduled soon after, which lasted for 2 hours. In the induction program, we were provided information about the company HCL and also ILP, which was an initial learning program. All the freshers have to go through this program, which is a training period before they are ready to work on real projects. The training program was made to strengthen the freshers and make them technically strong with their technical skills and soft skills, and also know about the company culture and its working process. We were also assigned a mentor for every 10 freshers who would guide us through our entire training period. We can stay in touch with mentors easily if there are any doubts or concerns. Furthermore, we had a top-notch program and all the freshers sitting there were overwhelmed with great energy and contentment. HCL was one of the most popular companies to begin one's corporate journey.

That was it, after the induction program was ended. We were given the option to choose a bank out of 5 different choices for our salary account. It was a mandatory process to open a salary account with any of the given listed banks so that the company can pay us the salary. After doing all the documentation work and approvals, I strolled out of the office to the cafeteria with my brand-new friends Rohan and Kreepesh, we were all very thrilled and filled with excitement. I made an effort to have a chat with some other freshers, but I can only get along well with Rohan and Kreepesh, although both had very different qualities.

We were provided information that the training period would last around 1 month. I had my lunch at the cafeteria along with Rohan and Kreepesh where we exchanged our contact numbers and followed each other on social media accounts and then headed back to our respective staying places.

I headed back to Soha PG…..

7

May 2018, Noida

After a month.......

Let's live our lives to the fullest, guys, Rohan barked in jubilation. Rohan Gupta and Kreepesh Sharma were my only two friends in Delhi. They were working in my office in HCL. Rohan was of average build and stood around 5 feet 7 inches tall, brown-skinned young man but took exceptional care to make himself appear good and develop his personality. He was born and raised in a small town in Bihar. He was a wicked guy. Kreepesh Sharma was from the city of Kolkata, slightly taller and fairer than Rohan and slimmer, and he was the sort of person who was very committed to his career because of his dire financial condition. I was taller than both at around 5 feet 10 inches, wheatish white complexion, and way more handsome than many added with an attractive personality. I was placed in HCL at Rs 10 Lakhs per annum package as Software Developer, Rohan at 8 lakhs per annum as Software Engineer Trainee and Kreepesh at 5 lakhs per annum as Test Engineer. We worked in different teams in the office.

I stayed in the Soha PG for nearly one month and I have gotten to know both Rohan and Kreepesh for these one month, and we bonded pretty well and frequently used to chill out together during our office hours in our HCL campus. Knowing that Rohan was from Bihar, we nurtured a strong bond together. We were all new to Delhi, and we stayed in our respective PG's at different locations before we shifted to our flats. Once we got comfortable in Delhi, we decided to rent a 3BHK flat for all three of us to stay together. The rent of the flat was Rs, 30000 per month and the flat was at a 2 km walking distance from the HCL office in the same place where Soha PG was located in Raipur Khadar, Sector 126, Noida, and it was a very spacious flat. The only drawback was that we had to cook our food, and neither of us had done that before.

The neighborhood appeared calm and peaceful, with a picturesque view of the corporate buildings outside. The Raipur Khadar area was full of boys and girls PG's, and flats. There were many cafés in and around the area. We assembled all the gas Chulhas, cylinders, dust bin and other cooking equipment to cook our food in our flat. We eventually gave up cooking just after a few days, and we decided to hire a maid to prepare our food since it was not a PG but a flat and neither of us were experienced in making food and due to office work, it was almost impossible for us to cook food with such fatigued hands that used to type the majority of the day on our laptops. However, we enjoyed having chai and snacks together and got to the top floor, which was more than a rooftop for us and enjoyed a glorious overview of the place. We shared laughs and cracked jokes more often than not, and we were having some real entertaining moments altogether in a lovely city and yes, with our own salary that was really enriching.

After two weeks.......

It was close to 9 AM. I along with Rohan and Kreepesh were on foot heading with our office bags to our office and were desperate to have some breakfast nearby since our maid was only available to cook lunch and dinner and no breakfast. She was a 40-year-old businesswoman rather than a maid and earned around Rs 30000 as salary by working as a maid in 5 flats altogether. She desires to work for male bachelors only to deceive them simply because male bachelors don't have any idea of cooking and food, it was easy for her to dupe male bachelors, and we already knew that, but we had no other options at that point. During this two weeks, we often used to eat food by ordering it online, and she took full advantage of it, she knew it in a very short span of time that if she gets absent, we would order the food online and she more often than not made bogus excuses to be absent from work. We never told her that we will deduct the daily amount if she gets absent from the salary that was Rs 6000 per month we used to give her for cooking food for 3 people, and she was aware of that. Our only point of concern was having morning breakfast while going to the office and tea, of course, along with evening meals. We were on the hunt for some nearby cafés or restaurants which can serve us some breakfast, and we can also have our morning tea together.

After walking over 800 meters from our flat, we ended up at 'Agarwal Cafe which was located in Raipur Khadar, Sector 126 itself' and the menu board that was installed just beside the café stated that it serves tea, coffee and morning breakfast and beverages as well. Apart from that, it also served lunch. I can't live without tea, and it was very important for me to find a nearby café that served tea, breakfast was secondary to me. There were a bunch of people already having their breakfast. We were hoping it would be a good café. We speedily got to the café and inquired about chai and breakfast. The café did appear lovely, it was well-maintained and elegantly decorated with lights, and there was a lot of crowding of customers who were mostly young working people wanting to have their breakfast because it was an office hour.

We asked for a cup of chai and 'chole bhature' as our breakfast from the teenage boy who was roaming around and taking orders. I rolled my eyes around and noticed that the built-up area of the café was around 1500 square feet. The café looked fabulous with sleek and modern interiors designed with wooden accents. There were more than 10 employees in the café, one was this teenage boy who was taking orders from customers. There were two managers who overseen the café's operations and ensured that everything runs smoothly. There were 3 baristas who were skilled in crafting special coffee drinks. Two skilled chefs who prepared delicious breakfast and lunch items. Three servers who took orders and served customers. One who sat at the billing counter and took the payments. The café provided sitting areas both inside and outside. People can even have their breakfast and lunch sitting in an open area outside. There were more than 10 tables kept outside for this purpose. To me, it was the best café. The café looked like an already, incredibly, established café, and it served more than 200 menu items altogether for breakfast and lunch, including more than 10 flavors of tea such as Adrak tea, ilachi tea, green tea, normal tea, chocolate tea, black tea, tandoori tea, butter tea and others.

I really enjoyed this place Rohan, it looks beautiful and cozy, what do you say? I asked Rohan, overjoyed.

Yeah, this place looks good enough to spend some quality time here, Rohan added, exhibiting his glistening white teeth.

What do you mean by quality time, Rohan, I rolled my eyes and asked, confused.

I mean look at the environment guys, there is a lot of buzz here, a lot of positive energy flowing through, What a view, Rohan said, twirling his eyes to all the girls around to both of us, I and Kreepesh.

We are not here to spend quality time and just stare at girls Rohan, please keep in mind we are here to do our job and build our career, Kreepesh said in a bit of a frustrated tone.

We angled our eyes at him and gave him a wicked look.

Also, look up at the pricing of the café, it's expensive, and I am not a millionaire like you both, there are a lot more other cafés that can serve reasonably priced breakfast, and we are not here for some enjoyment but to nourish our career, he added and he threw a taunt.

Okay, hold on guys, don't argue with each other, let's have our chai and breakfast. I became the middleman man to silent things. I already knew Rohan was that classic tharki guy and his view was different from everyone. I decided to change the topic of the discussion.

I was sitting outside and was enjoying having my breakfast at the café, and then all of a sudden, I sensed a flash of lightning. It was not a thunderstorm, but a beauty storm. A charming, beautiful girl, wheatish-white complexioned, with long straight brown hair drooping down to her waist, dark Kajal encircled in her eyes, wearing a pair of sparkling white rounded earrings, and an eye-catching luminous lip color got off from her scooty and made her way into the Café walking like a model on a ramp walk throwing her hands in the air and swinging her hair. She turned her eyes towards me and glided past me, revealing her hourglass figure. As I shifted my eyes towards her, the keys of my eyelids got lost, making my eyeballs permanently locked at her natural beauty. I rubbed my eyes and I could see her taking her seat which appeared like a throne where the queen was ready to take her place and get worshiped.

'*bijli girane main hoon aayi*', Rohan sang this song. "*kehte hai tujhko hawa hawai*", I completed the remaining lyrics of the song. I could have written an entire engineering paper on her beauty, and even the professor would have loved to read my paper.

The most striking part was that when she got to the café, she took the chair at the billing counter and sat down and started collecting the Bill amount from the customers. We speculated that she could either be the owner of the Agarwal café or the daughter of the owner.

Rohan Gupta was one of our 'kanjoos' friends who always hesitated while paying whenever we had something together. He had always tried his best to save money for mutual funds. But that day, even he was willing to make that payment for all three of us to look Cool In front of her. We rushed to the reception to make the payment. I had to rush, and I got there faster than my two other friends could.

How much is the bill? I asked her with a pleasant smile, looking straight into her eyes.

Your table no please, she responded in a very melodious tone.

Table no 9 outside one, this was our table no in the outside area where we all three had our breakfast, I responded back.

Rahul, send me the bill for outside table no 9, she pointed out the teenage boy.

Rahul brought in the bill, and she printed the bill from her Computer and handed it to me with a QR code attached to the bill for making the payment.

I looked at the bill, flaunted my iPhone X making sure my logo was clearly visible to her and scanned the QR code for the payment. She passed me a smile, a good smile. I was still intently staring at her and I got lost for some time and then came to my sense when she interrupted, your payment is received.

I took shorter steps and walked sluggishly to Rohan and Kreepesh, who were excitedly waiting for my return, before we made our way to our HCL Office.

.....

8

"She is your bhabhi guys", I reminded both Rohan and Kreepesh. After eating morning breakfast at Agarwal café for the first couple of days. We were very rest assured that we will have all our future tea, snacks, and breakfast at Agarwal Cafe only. Our office was at 10 AM, we decided to go to Agarwal café twice in a day, during the morning while going to the office and in the evening while returning from the office. We mostly covered this distance on foot. Surprisingly, just after a few days, Kreepesh was no longer interested in accompanying us to the café precisely because he did not like Rohan squinting his eyes at the girls and all over the café and having a 360-degree view around and also the expensive pricing of the café. It seemed like he was getting annoyed for no reason. We could easily sense it from his ragged voice.

However, the scooty girl which I was adhering to used to come to the café during the evening at around 7 PM. We got aware of this after several visits to the café. We suspected that the first day, there could possibly be some other reasons that she was seen in the morning. Thereafter, we could only see her in the evening at the café. In the morning, I could see another guy who was taller, wheatish complexioned, wearing rectangular spectacles running the café, we guessed he could possibly be her brother, although there was no similarity between him and the girl. There was not much to do for us during the morning. We normally had our tea and breakfast, and then we got moving quickly within 5 minutes on the way to our office.

My office used to shut at 6 PM every day, and I would take an extra half an hour to reach the Agarwal café, most likely with Rohan. We were aware that the girl will be arriving around 7 PM, so we had to make some adjustments, we had to loiter around here and there to soak up that extra half an hour. Furthermore, Rohan used to twirl his eyes to get some views there. We would giggle, crack some idiotic jokes and make fun of each other during that time. I was familiar with the surname of the girl, that was Agarwal. It was of the utmost importance for me to find her real name as soon as I possibly could. I liked her, and I wanted to make her mine, she was only mine.

We were engaged in some discussion, and I widened my eyes and I gazed at her black scooty. My eyes lit up, and my cheeks became bright red like a tomato. I was staring at her in full seriousness. She was dressed in a red color beautiful kurti. My eyes glowed red from black. She applied brakes with her legs, which made a lurching sound, and got down from her scooty. She carried her helmet in her hands, and she headed towards her throne where she used to sit every evening, i.e. at the billing counter.

I sprinted towards the café like an excited dog, leaving Rohan behind at a blistering speed. She had already taken her throne. I was stunned to see her beauty. Her long and lustrous silky hair made me her fan, she was a celebrity to me. In fact, more than a celebrity.

'*Pyar tera pyar Mujhe kiche Teri ore*', I went straight to her.

I ordered a special tandoori chai for me and also for Rohan, who was hovering at a certain distance near to the table no 9 and gave her a warm stare, she understood that I was so much into her. I yearned to communicate with her, but my inner self did not allow me. I liked her. I was tempted to ask her name and know more about her, but I could not. All I did was to sit at table no 9 outside the café that gave me a direct side view of her since the billing counter was located just outside the café and not inside. *She looked beautiful from all the geographical angles.*

Just as I was glancing at her, I remembered our HOD's words, never get involved with girls. What if the girl is a celebrity, I thought to myself.

I was deeply attracted to her. Rohan, as expected, was very busy having an entire view of the café having a cup of chai in his hand. There was a lot of hubbub that energized Rohan. My only chain of thoughts going in my mind was to figure out her real name as soon as possible so that I can find out her social media accounts and then plan my game further, but I had no courage to ask her name straight away or to have any sort of communication with her since she used to mind her work mostly and did not interact much with the customers who were interested in talking to her.

This continued, and We spent around one month at that tea café, and I was still unknown to her name: I was only known to the fact that she was also a great chai lover like me. She used to arrive, sit and order her a special chai. I had seen so many tea cups around her at the billing counter. It's a great idea to have tea at your own shop rather than paying someone else. I liked the business.

Every day, I visited the tea café twice without any failure, had tea, saw her and made myself blissful, stared at her from a distance, paid the bill amount and made my way to my flat. It was important for me to at least have some conversation with her at any cost. Even though I was an engineer, I would not mind engaging in any cyber crime to get to know her name and social media accounts. I was ready for all.

Occasionally, I could even sense that she was also looking at me. I confirmed it with Rohan, as he said when I don't look at her, she looks at me: My hormones were super excited after listening to all these words from Rohan. But what if she is only making sure whether I am staring at her or not? I thought to myself.

One more thing that I witnessed was that whenever I made the payment at the billing counter, there were a lot of other young guys too around me who were queued up to pay the bill, and she used to call most of them *bhaiya*, similarly like '*bhaiya aapka itna bill hua*', but she never called me '*bhaiya*' and I was like why did not it linger in my mind before. Is she interested in me? Does she like me too? Why can't she call me Bhaiya? I was bombarding myself with several questions.

That day I returned to my flat and could not sleep for the whole night. I tossed and turned for the entire night. I was still wondering why she does not call me *bhaiya* and this never touched my mind before, it came to my mind that day and this was true. She used to call everyone *bhaiya*, but not me. I directed an entire movie in my imaginary world with me and her. Although your name is unknown, but I will find it soon my future girlfriend, I promised to myself.

I blushed and turned around with a pillow in my arms.......................

9

July 2018

"Common Aarav, ask her name directly, I banged my fist on the wall, and encouraged myself.

It was close to three months that I was here in Noida, and it was 2 months of regular visits to Agarwal Cafe, and I was still struggling to find her name. My training period in my company was wrapped up a long ago, and I was currently working on real projects. There was a lot of pressure as a fresher while handling those projects.

Rohan, as expected, was not bothered about anything and Kreepesh was more engrossed in his career building and I can sympathize that he wanted a good life for himself. The only dilemma for Kreepesh was that he was poor at his verbal communication skills, which was creating problems for him in the office and collaborating on projects, and he was looking in great stress from the past few weeks. We tried everything to uplift Kreepesh, but we could not. Time went by, and we continued with our visit to the Agarwal café.

One fine day.

I was returning from my office, and I was very disheartened and desperate at the same time to know her name, nothing had changed, it was nothing more than glancing and gazing at each other for the past two months. I did not have yet even made a 10-minute continuous interaction with her. I got bummed out. In the past few months, I have tried 1000 different kinds of tactics and techniques to get her name and account on social media, but I could not succeed. Only Black magic was left. I was losing patience. I asked Rohan for some ideas.

Ask her directly Aarav, I am sure she is genuinely interested in you, I can promise you that, Rohan suggested with absolute confidence in his voice.

And what if she gets pissed off and creates a scene and kicks me out of her café, I responded, to Rohan, with a sense of nervousness and hesitancy. I won't be then able to see her again, I added.

Then probably you are wasting your time, Aarav, what if someone else approaches her before you do. Even if you get to know her social media profiles, you still have to interact with her to move it forward, be courageous and ask her name, Rohan took a dig at my manliness.

We were fully engaged in our serious discussion and at that moment, my phone rang which was a missed call from an unknown number which I did not bother to respond to; however, my eyes gazed at the phone clock, and It was already around 7 PM. I moved my foot forward to make my way to the café. While I was interacting with Rohan, I focused my eyes from a certain angle and I could figure out that she was on her way to the café with her scooty from a long distance. This time I used the ultra zooming camera of my iPhone X to track her. As she came closer to us, I noticed that she was not alone, there was also a girl who was sitting behind her on her scooty. I thought that maybe she was her friend.

She drove closer to the café and, as usual, applied the brakes with her legs. The girl had been sitting behind her, got down from the scooty. Trust me, I had no interest in looking at her, and I did not. But Rohan seized the opportunity to full extent and rolled his eyes. She was a short girl, likely around 5 feet, slightly wheatish complexioned and had short black hair. She wore high heels to look taller. Mrs. Agarwal dressed herself in a black one-piece dress, and she walked in towards the café to take her usual throne, and we rushed to order.

Swaaatiii...., take your bag, the girl cried out from a long distance.

Ohh sorry, she waved her hand and made a gesture to the girl, and she ran to her to take her bag back.

Ohhh Swati, I turned my face and flicked my eyes towards Rohan in great excitement.

She carried the bag and came back to her seat while the girl took off somewhere before we could figure it out, but I did not bother to investigate further. She had never come with bags before, but that day she had her bag and also that girl sitting behind, I suspected there might be some evening party or plans for them or a birthday party, who knows. Anyway, I was overjoyed to know that her name was Swati, and she was Swati Agarwal. This was all I needed to know to break the door of her social media accounts. I gave a cunning look to Rohan, and he understood what I was trying to convey through my eyes that were full of love.

I sprinted to her, and I ordered masala chai that day for us, and we were having chai as usual sitting on table no 9 that gave me a direct view of her from a distance while she was busy doing some work on her computer along with processing payments from customers. However, she looked in a hurry, as if she was desperate to finish her pending work as soon as possible. God knows what work she was doing on her computer.

Meanwhile, I was familiar with her name, I ordered Rohan to do a social media scan of Swati Agarwal and find her real I'd. We both searched for her name on Instagram, Facebook, multiple times, but we could not find her account. We experimented with multiple combinations of her name while searching, but still could not get to her account. Lastly, I even searched for her on Google thinking that she is not less than a celebrity for me, but could not find her either. I got heartsick, I was unable to not find anything related to her. Even after knowing her full name, her business name and all sort of things, still we were struggling to find her social media accounts. I guessed she might not be on social media. But my heart was not ready to accept this.

I tried so many other unsuccessful attempts to get her social media accounts but only to disappoint myself. Soon my glum face was brightened with glee when, Rohan reported to me that she was intently staring at me while I was busy on the lookout for her account snooping into my phone, and I could hear these lyrics from nowhere *'kala jadu Kare, lambe baal tere, aankhen Jheel Teri, Dore laal kare'*….

I blushed in excitement......

It was done for the day, I was hopeless, and I strolled to the billing counter to pay my bill amount with a hope that I could see her closely and simply look at her that would be enough for the day. I moved slowly to pay the bill amount. Meanwhile, the girl who came with her on scooty came back charging in. She was soaked in sweat, and she went straight to Swati.

Ridhi, why are you so late, It's more than 7:30 PM, and we are getting late, Swati raised her voice in anger.

I saw Swati fuming for the first time in my life, and she looked more charming when she was angry. It felt like Her angry lips were chirping some melodious song which was soothing to the ears. How can someone look so attractive even when they are angry, I thought to myself.

Ridhi Ahuja is never late baby, she is on time, she explained to Swati about her late arrival.

Don't you ever call her baby, I was about to scold Ridhi but kept my mouth locked up. I was not a jealous guy, but I got jealous hearing baby from someone's else mouth.

Swati picked up her bag and left on her scooty with Ridhi. She did not even bother to take the bill payment from me. Is she even interested in me? I quizzed myself with several questions. This made me disappointed. After failing to get her social media account, I planned to search for her friend Ridhi Ahuja's social media account, and then we can find her profile too. We were sure what our next move was. I orientated my face towards Rohan, and he understood what was our next assignment. We were used to doing team work as engineers in our projects, and here we needed collective effort as well.

The search began again............

10

"How is this even possible' are they from the ancient age", I burst out in disbelief when I came to know that even Ridhi was not on social media. I rushed to the door of my flat, slammed it with my leg to open it, I raced to my room and threw my office bag on my bed and right away started searching for Ridhi Ahuja once again on social media accounts, Facebook and Instagram. At the same time, I instructed Rohan and Kreepesh to do the same. All of them got into the task of figuring out her social media account. I immediately began to search for Ridhi on Facebook and Instagram with different name combinations and city name but could not find her I'd anywhere. I double-checked it, but once again I could not find any clues. I got annoyed and banged my fist on the bed. I could not believe that, even in this modern age, they were not using social media. I was not willing to accept that, and I speculated that there might be some other name for them on their social handles to hide their identity from their relatives or family members. I was scratching my head now. I forced myself to drink a glass of water to cool myself.

I was looking for any leads from Rohan and plopped down again on my bed to find Ridhi's ID, but only to dishearten myself. I was frustrated, and all my excitement of getting to know Swati's real name was going out of the window now. My body was no longer producing feel good hormones, and I was worried.

Just before giving up for the final time, I did a search for Ridhi again on Instagram and added her favorite word, **'baby'** which she used to call Swati with. I did a search for **'Ridhi baby'** and I erupted with happiness and delight when I got to find her real ID. Her ID was __**ridhibaby**__. It was she and her profile Pic featured her wearing black sunglasses, and she was with Swati showing off her beautiful pout from behind. The sight of Swati on her DP energized my body with eagerness to know more. Her account was public, and I found several new and old photos of her with Swati and her other friends.

Her Instagram bio was,
Ridhi
Sweet baby
BCom….

Now the whole thing was getting clearer. She did graduation in BCOM. I went to her following list and searched for Swati Agarwal but could not track down any followings related to Swati Agarwal. I typed Swati in the search box of her following and I found my celebrity, her I'd was just __**swati**__ and there was no surname that was added to it. And no surname was the reason I could not track her social media accounts anywhere. I was still wondering why did they both not add their surname anywhere. This looked like a mystery.

Swati's account was private; her stunning DP was still visible to me where she was posing with her scooty at her café. I was unable to stop myself from smiling. I was feeling a great sense of exuberance and joy that emanated within me and spread through my entire body. She was also a Bcom graduate, as mentioned in her bio. I guessed both Swati and Ridhi were college friends. I got trapped in my own imaginary world. My hormones got up to their feet again, and I sprinted with wider steps to Rohan and Kreepesh to share the good news.

Guys, you know what, there is good news to share with you all, I addressed them with the happiest tone I have ever spoken with.

And what's that Aarav, Rohan asked as he turned his eyes towards me.

Is it related to Swati or something else? Kreepesh asked confusedly.

Guys, I found Ridhi's Instagram I'd and also Swati's, I barked in excitement and went straight to Rohan and Kreepesh to reveal my phone and their ID only to get them to know that this news was real, and I was not joking.

Congratulations Aarav, it's party time, Rohan saluted my hard work and hugged me. Kreepesh shared a warm smile as he looked towards me and Rohan hugging like newly married couples.

It's party time guys, I am offering a grand party for all of you, I declared in extreme joy.

Did you send her follow request Aarav, Rohan inquired.

Not yet yaar, I don't have any good recent pictures of mine, I will click some handsome new pics of mine and then upload it to my DP and then send her follow request, What do you say Rohan, I asked Rohan for some ideas and suggestions.

So you will spend your hard-earned money unnecessarily on a party only to take good pictures of yours so that you can showcase it to Swati? Am I right Aarav, at least respect money, she had already seen you in person, how much will a good DP matter to her, Kreepesh threw an entire passage of his motivational speech.

It's okay, Kreepesh, we should sometimes enjoy, Rohan and I cracked a joke and cooled down Kreepesh. The glow of joy could easily be seen in my eyes.

I made my way straight inside my room, opened my clothes, took a towel and hurried towards my washroom to take a good nude bath. I headed to the washroom and turned on the shower and threw my towel. I was enjoying a nice cold shower and then my hormones got enlivened again, and I started dancing and singing with utmost excitement while bathing.

Kabhi toh kisi ki dulhaniya banogy, mujhse Shadi krogy?? I sang this song in a loud voice.

I enjoyed a good nude bath and I came back to my room, combed my hair, applied some face creams and lotions and toggled on my sound box. I did not eat any food that day as I lost my appetite because of over excitement. I mumbled all the romantic songs of my playlist that day. However, I could not sleep all night and was reminiscing about Swati and only Swati. All that I did that night was to simply toss and turn without any sleep. I tried hard to sleep because there was my office in the next morning, but I could not.

11

Get ready guys, we are getting late, I was screaming at both Rohan and Kreepesh for unreasonably causing the delay. It was Sunday afternoon at around 5 PM, and we had an off day from the office, and we were getting ready to head out to Cirrus 9 - The Oberoi, which was a well-known rooftop restaurant and bar. I ended up choosing this restaurant because it gave a fabulous view of the entire city, and it had some truly astonishing vibes. I adored the background scene, and I was confident that my pictures snapped here would most certainly be liked by Swati. My motive was to capture some cool, good-looking pictures of mine with a picturesque background scene setting and upload it as my DP on Instagram before I can send Swati follow request.

'pehli nazar mei kaisa jaadu kar diya, tera ban baitha hai mera jiya', I sprinted towards the mirror of my room.

I ran towards my mirror and took a glance at my overall appearance and personality, I dressed in a slightly grayish cargo pants and a black fit shirt. I opted to wear a black color shirt because I looked really handsome in black and used to get a lot of attention from people. Moreover, I wore on a stylish watch and a black color shoes that paired perfectly with my shirt, drizzled my favorite perfume and altered my hairstyle for the final time before I made my way to Rohan's room where both Rohan and Kreepesh were dressing like brides. It wasn't clear to me why were they taking so much time to get ready. I pleaded with both of them to get ready as soon as possible so that we can reach the Cirrus 9 on time before dusk. I preferred to take my pictures in some natural light rather than in complete darkness. Kreepesh, as always, was a bit reluctant to go to the bar initially since he knew I was only going to the bar to pose for pictures and there was no other reason. He argued that it was just a squandering of hard-earned money. Rohan was overjoyed to enjoy the scenery and surroundings of the place. After a few minutes of haggling and then cracking some jokes, we moved out of our flat, booked a cab and quickly headed to Cirrus 9. The distance to the rooftop restaurant and bar from our flat was close to 15 kilometers, and it took us 45 minutes to reach our destination.

It was close to 6 PM, and we got to the Cirrus 9. I lifted my eyes to take a closer look at the entire bar and restaurant. With an impeccable location in the heart of the capital city, the ultra-modern bar was a hot favorite with its well-heeled patrons. It was surrounded by the lush greenery of the Delhi Golf Club, with the historic 16th-century Humayun's Tomb located a stone's throw away. Slightly further, but clearly visible to the eyes, were the majestically lit Rashtrapati

Bhawan, India Gate, and other iconic monuments that together make up the modern city of New Delhi. It was a picture-perfect restaurant.

We seated ourselves in our designated seats at the left corner of the bar that provided us a wonderful view in the background and decided to order some starters along with a beer or two, and coffee was mandatory for me. I deliberately spent half an hour only to convey to people around me that I was interested in the restaurant, and I was not here just for shooting pictures. After a few more minutes, I felt that this was the right time for me to execute my plans and take some perfect picture shots.

I stood up and grabbed kreepesh with me at the extreme end corner of the rooftop bar, where several tables were set up and a small group of people were posing for pictures around. It was mostly couples, both married and unmarried. That end of the bar gave a stupendous overview of the entire city. The place was idyllic, but still not as lovely as Swati. I asked Kreepesh to take some pictures of mine as he was the one who had top-notch skill sets of photography, and he often captured stunning pictures. I posed like a struggling model trying so many styles and positions and Kreepesh shot some outstandingly cool pictures of mine, and I was extremely impressed with his skills. Despite that, I still urged him to take a few more pictures for my future use as well as I was paying for the entire bill and if I didn't get a couple of decent pics, it shall be a great injustice to me. Kreepesh took some 20 pictures of mine in several styles, and then he handed over the phone to me to snap his own pics. Rohan too joined him. Soon, Rohan got frustrated and replaced me with Kreepesh as a cameraman after he discovered that I was taking his absolute worst pictures of all time. They both were unaware of the fact that I was never asked to shoot anyone's pictures, as I was the worst cameraman ever. My fingers were only good at coding and not clicking pictures.

My job was done now, and I was not enamored in the bar any more or the ambiance of the place. The picture of Swati was consistently huddling inside my head. We had our food, ate it pretty well, drank some beer and it was bill time. I gestured the manager to bring the bill. Just After 10 minutes, he handed over the bill to me with a QR code and card scanner. I scanned the QR code and paid the bill amount instantly.

We left the restaurant soon after, booked a cab and made our way back to our flat.

It was just before 11 PM, and I was anxiously picking out the best pic out of those 20 photos Kreepesh clicked. I was scrubbing my head, evaluating what if Swati does not like this pic or that pic. I was engaged in this work for the past one hour. I finally mustered some courage and settled on the two best pics out of those 20 pics where I considered myself smart and good-looking according to me, and I was certain Swati would like it too.

I uploaded one of my pics as mine Instagram DP and the second pic as a post on my profile. In both the pics, I felt super sexy and luscious. The next task was to delete all the previously uploaded pics where I was not looking good or might send a bad message to her. I deleted so many previously posted photos in my profile and Now my profile was almost ready dressed as a groom to send my future bride Swati a follow request. In my mind, it was not just a mere follow request but a genuine online rista from my side to her. I edited my bio and added software engineer at HCLTech to let her know the company where I was working.

I was not a smoker, but I plugged in a cigarette and smoked it to build up some courage and send Swati Agarwal follow request on Instagram. It was just after 12 PM, and I was thinking that she might have slept, so I realized it's not good to send her request at that moment as she might be sleeping. Should I send the request Tomorrow early in the morning or should I send it in the evening in the presence of her while having tea at her café, I pestered myself with several questions. I ultimately decided to send the follow request and go to bed and see what comes up the other day.

12

I fell asleep for a few minutes and I dreamt of Swati being dressed as a bride. I was enjoying the dream, but abruptly woke up when I noticed that I was nowhere present at her wedding. I got frustrated and scratched my head. Not being able to sleep, I spent my entire night tossing and turning more than a hundred times. I barely slept, even for an hour. All throughout the night I was just imagining about her and pestering myself questions with 'what if she does not accept my follow request, that worried me. I was also intrigued when I thought, what if she accepted my request. I had decided to turn off my phone that night in nervousness to avoid frequent checking of her Instagram account and the status of the request.

After a very stressful last night, It was right around 8 AM the next day, and my alarm bell jingled, I promptly turned off my alarm bell and wakened up to switch on my Phone. Before doing that, I chugged some water from my bottle which was kept just beside my bed and tugged on the power button to switch on my phone. I anxiously enabled my mobile data on. As soon as I enabled my mobile data, my phone was inundated with plenty of notifications from different sources and my heartbeat ran faster than an athlete. I squinted my eyes for a while and relaxed my heartbeat to settle in. I had no patience to check all the notifications, I straight away opened the Instagram app.

I looked at my Instagram account and shifted my eyes towards the notification icon. There were a few notifications which I hastened to click.

Swati wants to follow you, confirm or delete? Asked the Instagram notification.

Dear Instagram, please ensure you remove the delete button from someone amazingly beauteous like Swati whenever she sends someone a follow request. She is so gorgeous that her follow request does not deserve to be deleted, please keep that In mind, I had a suggestion for Instagram.

I quickly clicked on the Confirm button more Than 5 times to confirm that the request had been successfully accepted. She had already accepted my follow request. I refreshed my notification feed a dozen times to double-confirm it. I got into her account and There were 10 pretty pictures of her. I also came across some pictures of Ridhi Ahuja on her profile. An hour elapsed, and it was close to 9 AM, and I was still curled up somewhere in Swati's profile, I scrolled through her profile 100 times as if I had never seen her before.

'Dekha hazaro dafa apko, phir ye bekarari kaisi hai', I craned my eyes towards her DP.

I got the thumbs-up now, Rohan was right, if Swati was not genuinely interested in me at all, why would see request to follow me back at all. Why such a charming girl should care about me? She might already have a big line of people like me who adore her and who are eager to woo her. I felt that there is definitely something for me in her heart. I reminded myself of one of my close friends words when I was studying in my college that "beautiful girls don't approach guys even if they like them and that's the universal truth". I wasn't sure if that might be the case here too.

It was close to 9:15 AM, and I was running late for the office. I had to rush to the washroom to finish my shower and was dancing with full ferocity while bathing. I came back scurrying in to my room and I got myself dressed quickly in my formal, carried my laptop and bag and walked out. That day I chose to skip the Agarwal café only because I was feeling anxious and nervous and all I had wanted was to enjoy this sensation of joy which I got that day. I straight away went to my office.

That day, I was so overjoyed at my office that even my colleagues could not fathom why was I acting in such an immature way. I was not coding programs, but I was, in fact, coding Swati. Her eyes seemed like variables to me that were constantly located in my heart, Her nose, and lips appeared like data types, I wanted to typecast her angelic face to my heart, but I got stumped at my decision-making remembering her adorable expressions. Her natural beauty was whirling in my head in a loop for a while.

I got reconnected to my senses when one of my colleagues interrupted me. I had to hurry to complete all my remaining work for the project I was working on. After missing her for almost 8 hours, It was time to see her. It was just after 7 PM, and I was just about to leave my office; However, I got a little late at work that day because of my recent project. It was close to 7:30 PM and I headed to the café alone that day, since I was late and Rohan and Kreepesh had already left. To my pleasant surprise, the café was getting closed that day and I could see Swati wandering out of the café and some workers were huddled together. I suspected there was some remodeling going on their café. I speculated that they might renovate their café much more for customers attraction. I was in love with her business ideas now.

This is your chance Aarav, go and talk to her, I picked up some strength and headed straight to her.

Is the café closed today, I asked her with a very tender, dulcet tone and a serene expression on my face.

Yes, we are renovating it, it will remain closed from 7 PM for the next 5 days or even more. She informed me, giving a slight stare at me.

I got lost for a few seconds after finding myself in direct contact with her. She was attired in a red kurti and jeans, and I saw her eyes encircled with dark Kajal. When she spoke close to me, I ended up having a painless mini heart attack and after stroking my heart with my hands. I spoke to her again.

Oh, so I won't be able to have my favorite chai for the next 5 days, I responded to her with a regretful look on my face.

Can be more than 5 days, right? I stammered this time.

She blushed, Oh so you can't live without your chai, she inquired in a very melodic tone that softened my ears.

Yes it's true, I said to her, I like this place and the chai here is 'swatiest'. In fact, I have never sipped this kind of chai ever before in my life, I deliberately said 'swatiest' instead of sweetest and I stared at her flirtatiously.

What did you just say, did you say swatiest, she giggled as she turned her face towards me.

I said the sweetest chai, I repeated my sentence.

You seem to be a very funny guy, she responded, exhibiting her exquisitely glistening white teeth.

Yes, some people say that I have an excellent sense of humor and my sixth sense is what that makes my overall personality much more appealing, I flaunted my qualities.

Is it like that, she spoke again? What's the reassurance that those people tell the truth, she was taking a dig at me.

I got lost for a few seconds. I enjoyed her sense of humor.

Did you drink your chai today, she inquired again as she stared at me.

I cannot get it here now, I will have it somewhere. I responded.

The café will remain closed only after 7 PM, you can visit and have your sweetest chai before that, my brother will look after the café, she spoke sweetest with a lot more energy deliberately, it felt like she was teasing me.

We already knew each other's names, and we were also followers of each other on Instagram, but we did not talk about Instagram anything, not even a single word about it.

I got to go now, my brother would be on his way to take a look at the unfinished work, she grinned and picked up her bag and helmet and settled on her scooty …

'*Keh doon tumhe ya chup rahu, Dil me mere aaj kya h*', I mumbled this song when I turned to look at her as she buckled her helmet and was about to accelerate her scooty. She looked so adorable.' *Jo bolo toh jaanu, guru tumko maanu, chalo ye bhi waada hai*', I sang the left-over lyrics while making my way back to my flat.

13

I was completely lost, and I had hooked up a headphone and was tapping my foot on the floor to some lovely romantic songs. It was close to 10 PM, and I was wholeheartedly immersed in Swati. I had no words of my own to praise her natural beauty. She was a queen. From the past few days, I have been struggling to maintain focus on my office work and that gave me headaches. I locked myself in my room, and I was so lost that I was not having any sort of conversation with even Rohan and Kreepesh, and that befuddled them. I only desired the café to open up as quickly as possible so that I can gaze at Swati. My adoration for her kept on growing and for The next five days; I scrolled through her Instagram profile more than 500 times even during my office hours and browsed her pictures more than 1000 times. I would be a topper who would have been placed at a minimum of 50 lakhs per annual package if I had studied my subjects like I was studying Swati, I thought to myself.

I carefully examined all her followings and followers in these 5 days: I was just curious to know about any relationship she might have in the past or even in the future or someone she likes. I was totally unaware of anything in her personal life. I did a good assessment of her profile through my wide open eyes and found nothing alarming that would break my heart.

It was just after 11 PM, and I had my dinner along with Rohan and Kreepesh, and I was lounging on my bed scrolling through her profile again. She uploaded a picture of herself in a stunning red suit, and I was like, how can someone be so beautiful in this kalyug. Her natural beauty should be protected, and I will be the protector. I quickened my hands to like her newly posted pic. I tried my best to cope with my emotions, but my hormones went into overdrive, and it impelled me to send the most dangerous and scary message you can ever send it to a beautiful girl.

I got myself fired up to send her a direct message.

I sent hi ......

After sending hi, I devoured all my calories walking to and fro in my room. I pulled on my headphone and roamed nervously all over my room. I trekked to Rohan's room, then to Kreepesh and vice versa, then came straight back to my room, moved to the terrace and then came back, went to the washroom more than 5 times and came all the way back to my room. I kept doing this for more than an hour, and I began to feel fatigued as I burned all my calories. I threw my headphones on the table and plopped on my bed. I cradled my Phone underneath my pillow.

After an hour, at around 12 AM, I stood up again, and I chugged in some water from my bottle, I picked up my phone and glanced at the screen. I saw the most beautiful notification Instagram can ever send me. I was so chuffed that even I decided to work for Instagram as a software engineer, all for free.

It was 'hi' from Swati …

I received the message, but I did not respond straightaway, I was aflutter and also nervous at the same time. The most arduous task is to push a communication forward after sending that hi. However, I derived some courage and I tried to move ahead with the conversation in my own way.

Will the café remain open Tomorrow? I messaged. She had previously informed me that day that the café would be closed for 5 days only in the evening, and Tomorrow was the sixth day. I considered raising this question to expedite my communication forward.

Yes, she gave an answer after 20 minutes. She was beautiful and beautiful girls have attitude, and they will respond late, I actually knew that universal fact.

Amazing, I texted back, with a smiley right after reading her message. I started to feel as if I have to control these hormones: It's spiraling out of control. She may think, I am fiddling with my phone only to respond to her message and that is likely to send a bad signal of mine to her.

Have a bit of patience, Aarav, I thought to myself. After a few minutes of silence, I got another text from her.

How did you find my Instagram ID ?, she asked with a cheeky emoji.

I was just missing a semicolon in my coding, once I figured out the semicolon, I was able to execute my code successfully.

What?? She asked in perplexity.

Actually, I just did a search for your name, and your ID popped up in the suggestions section, and then I sent you the follow request.

And how did you come to know my name? She lobbed a dynamite at me.

I was perplexed as to what to answer her, and then I chose to speak the truth. Actually, I heard Ridhi calling you Swati that day, and then I became aware of your name, I responded to her with a smiley.

Okay, she laughed, sharing an emoji and got offline.

She ended up offline for more than half an hour, and I was nervous. I was still glaring at my phone screen, expecting for her next message. I got jittery, thinking what if she might have got angry at me, what if she did not feel comfortable with me sending her follow request in a way that I did? I pelted myself with plenty of questions. I left my phone beside.

After a few minutes of waiting, I listened to a notification vibration and I hurriedly scooped up my phone.

But I will not be present for the next 7 days at my café, I am about to go on a Kerala trip with Ridhi and a couple of my other friends.

Her message settled my heart in, and I breathed a sigh of relief, but her idea of traveling to Kerala for a trip made me heartbroken. I was impatiently waiting to see her for these 5 very long days and I would not be able to see her for more 7 days. I was extremely upset, and I saw the text and I did not respond to it. After a couple of minutes, I got energized again as I mulled over why did she informed me that she will not be there at her café. Does she know that I head to her café only to look at her rather than sipping tea? I was bombarding myself with several reasonable questions. I got the hints from her already, and my hormones jumped up to their feet.

After A few minutes, she texted me another message.

You can still drink your sweetest chai at my café, my brother will be there. It almost seemed like she was teasing me again for that sweetest chai word which I had spoken to her earlier. She had honed in on that specific word. I couldn't stop myself from blushing.

She was teasing me and giving me signals, and was deliberately including the word sweetest in her text messages. Some of my ancient family members had played some cricket, and I had it in my genes too. I knew how to smack a full toss for six ...

Can I share with you something if You don't mind, please think of this as a gesture of appreciation, nothing else, I requested her.

Yes, please go on, she replied with an emoji.

You are so beautiful that this Kalyug does not deserve you, Please go back to somewhere where your natural beauty is worshiped. I picked up the full toss from her and smashed a six out of the stadium.

This was the very best pick-up line I could ever say it to her.

She broke out in laughter and sent me at least 10 guffawing emojis in response.

Miss.Swati, Ne'er ever toss a full toss to Aarav Tripathi, I mumbled to myself.

We exchanged a few more text messages just before it turned 1 o clock, and she said bye.

I greeted her with happy journey and set off to get some sleep; otherwise I would have ended up late for my next day in the office. I grabbed a pillow in my arms and rolled all over the bed in a state of excitement.

For the next few days, she was on her Kerala trip, and we carried on exchanging text messages on Instagram. Unfortunately, we could not have much of a conversation since I was caught up in my office hours, and she got busy on her Kerala trip. We went through the usual one: line messages that were centred around, where was my hometown, where was hers, how the café got started, and how did I get to HCL and all, but I was elated that I was able to talk to her. I also came to know the location of her house where she stayed. Her house was located in Sector 47 Noida, 5 km away from her café. I did not visit Agarwal café in the morning or evening for the next few days as I felt that there was no sense in spending time there since Swati was not over there and I simply liked swatiest chai and nothing else …

14

"Let's have breakfast at the Agarwal café, guys", Rohan pitched in. It was close to 9:30 AM, and we were already running late for our office. I had chosen not to go to the café in the evening or in the morning, as it did not make me feel good without Swati being there in the evening and

I did not like interacting with her brother. It was pointless for me. However, we were all feeling hungry and wanted to have breakfast before we could set off to our office. Rohan recommended having breakfast and tea at the Agarwal café, while Kreepesh shied away again because of the expensive pricing. He abandoned us in the mid-way to have his breakfast somewhere else at a reasonable price, while Rohan enticed me to go to the café. Rohan and I strolled to the café, leaving Kreepesh behind. While on my way to the café, I was deeply entwined in Swati's thoughts. I pulled up my phone and went through her profile again. I did find out that she had recently put up a few stories on her Instagram which I liked instantly, and she truly was looking astoundingly charming in those pictures. I was patiently waiting for her to share some posts of Kerala trip on her Instagram feed so that I can like it and give her some more hints. I was aware of my next moves quite well. I knew that Swati was also enamored with me as she would have not responded to my follow request which was very much an online Rista. In fact, she followed me back, and she responded to my text messages. She could have also ignored my messages, but she did not. She replied to each of my messages although late and also teased me with the swatiest word. She was cognizant that I liked her, and I had a smart plan in my head for my next steps.

With thousands of ruminations floating in my mind, Rohan and I finally got to the Agarwal café. Her brother was there and Rohan used to have a few conversations with her brother even in the past, particularly during morning hours when he was present. They got along well. The name of her brother was Abhay, and he stood at a height of slightly over 5 feet 10 inches, was slimmer, had a wheatish complexion, and wore a pair of glasses. He was elder to us, and elder to

Swati as well, but still, he and Rohan got on very well and used to have a lot of fun together. Despite this, I did not commune with Abhay at all because I felt a bit awkward around him since I liked Swati and my inner self did not allow me to talk to her brother as causally as I talk to other people. I was apprehensive. Rohan and I had our breakfast, and we made our way to the office.

How is it going with Swati Aarav? Is she responding, Rohan asked in an inquisitive tone.

Yes, I exchanged a couple of text chats with her, it was limited to hi and hello and not much, I responded to him as I shifted my face towards him.

Life should be like yours Aarav, a handsome guy placed at a good package and will also be dating a beautiful girlfriend at the same time, Rohan responded, and the facial expressions did not seem pleasant to me.

She is certainly not my girlfriend, Rohan, I shot back.

But She will be, I am sure she is interested in you, Rohan added.

I can't vouch for that Rohan whether she likes me or not, nor have I spoke to her much in person, and I don't know her in person, so I can't comment on anything at this point. We are mere followers on Instagram and nothing else, I responded.

You hang out with me all the time Aarav but still choose to evade things, that's strange, Rohan scoffed. I assumed he could possibly have spotted my over jovial mood in the past few days and had figured out there was something going in between me and Swati.

yaar Rohan, I am leaving now, I would rather not make it an issue Right now, even if she eventually decides to become my girlfriend, what's wrong in it? I spoke to Rohan, baffled, in a raspy tone.

There is absolutely nothing wrong Aarav, I was just curious to know more about my bhabhi, Rohan attempted to ameliorate my mood.

Rohan and I went straight to our office. However, for the first time in mine and Rohan's friendship, I felt a sense of jealousy. My manager used to love my work in my office, and I was progressing really well with my career, I was getting accolades, and I was very sure I would also have Swati in my life. I suspected that these all thing might have made Rohan wonder so much. Anyway, I decided to keep our friendship as healthy as possible.

That day was a very long day for me at my office, since I started mulling over more of mine and Rohan's discussions. I did not felt good enough. To cheer up my mood, I scrolled through Swati's profile and was avidly waiting for her to upload some adorable new pictures of her from her Kerala trip that would brighten up my whole day.

After a couple of hours, at around 2 PM, just after I had my lunch at my office. I discovered that Swati uploaded two new pictures with Ridhi on her Instagram feed. My body started jiggling in exuberance. I visualized my father demonstrating to me his bike engine power by throttling the accelerator, I saw myself sitting on his bike and pulling the accelerator at 120 km/hour: Yes, that was the speed with which I liked Swati's newly uploaded Instagram post. She flaunted her beautiful eyes and curved eyebrows in the pic. She looked so gorgeous in her black one-piece that I had to squint my eyes. She posted it just a few seconds ago, and I was the first one to like the post. I began to wonder what she might be thinking of me.

'*Tere mast mast do nain mere dil ka le Gaye chain*', I babbled this song in my office, turning on my chair.

15

"Why had Kreepesh chosen to do that, Rohan", I questioned Rohan in complete disbelief.

Rohan informed me that Kreepesh has left our flat and will settle in somewhere else in a shared room that is likely to cut down his monthly living expenses. He was upset because of his job stress, as he was having a hard time working on projects because of his poor communication skills. His family's financial condition has got more dire, and he opted to save his monthly salary to support his family.

'And what we are going to do now Rohan, our is a 3 Bhk flat, and we will be left with only both of us', I responded to Rohan dismayed.

He suggested, "should we move out of our flat and change into a 2 Bhk.

I can't allow myself to get settled in somewhere else, I have to stay in close proximity to the Agarwal café since I have to visit it daily, I responded to Rohan with a dejected gesture.

I can understand it Aarav, but I can't afford very high rent. I have to look after my family as well, it appeared that he was taunting me.

Rohan, if we can find a flat that is within 1 km distance of Agarwal café then I am fine with that; apart from that I would have no other choice, I told him.

That's fine, Aarav, we will come up with a solution, he responded with a certainty. Let's take a look online at some nearby 2 bhk flats, if available.

I nodded.

My excitement was morphed into worries now. I was chuffed that Swati was supposed to come back to Delhi from Kerala in only a couple of days, but Kreepesh decision to leave our flat irked me. I could not allow myself to go far away from Agarwal café, and it's very tough to get a new flat quick since it gets clogged quickly. I could just not stay in a 3bhk alone either, or even with Rohan, since it would get very overpriced to rent it for two people. Sooner or later, I have to start looking for a new flat, or I have to live alone somewhere else in a 1BHK or a PG. I was ensnared in a horrible situation.

After mulling over so much in my head, I started looking for some vacant flats in the close vicinity in Raipur Khadar, sector 126 only, but our current flat was in a decent place and was also spacious, and I could not find any similar flats. Struggling to find anything, I decided, to choose Swati over anything else. If I don't come to a solution, I will rather go back to a PG and stay alone if Rohan does not lend a hand, but I will not go far away from Swati and her café, I thought to myself, but I struggled to deal with my emotions.

It was around 11 PM and I had my dinner along with Rohan, and we both tried our best to let go of our tension by pulling off some jokes and that probably aided us in elevating our mood back to normal. We made promises to each other that we would most likely find some way or other. With a nice feeling, I came back to my room and flopped on my bed. I was actively fantasizing about Swati, I was excited that she would come back in a few days and I would be able to reconnect with her. Meanwhile, my wicked mind suggested" let's post a pic and see whether she likes the pic or not", if she likes the pic that conveys that she likes me. I picked up my phone and swiped for all the pics I had snapped in Cirrus 9, it were altogether 20 pics that were shot by Kreepesh, whom I was missing terribly. I managed to pick 2 top-notch photos and I posted it to my Instagram account and also to my Instagram story.

It was a little over 11:30 PM and I cradled my phone beside my pillow and was humming to some romantic songs to ameliorate my mood with a pair of earphones snuggled in my ears. I was awake, but I was in a dream. Just after a few minutes, I could sense a notification vibration and I instinctively hastened to hold my phone up. I was staring at my phone to see the wonderful notification. My eyes were glistening with love.

Swati liked your photo, I got a notification.

I rapidly clicked on the notification more than the speed of the Light to double-check it whether she had liked it or not or was I dreaming. This was my favorite day. I was convinced that she liked me as well. However, I did not have as much conversation with her in person as I would have liked, and I also did not know much about her family background other than that she has one brother and her father owns the café.

I browsed Swati's profile a few more times more and docked my phone to the charger. I wished for her to return from the Kerala trip as soon as possible, and I would have some interaction with her in person. Then things might progress forward, and she would most likely be mine girlfriend as she was only mine.

16

"Aaj mausam bada imaandar hai", I twisted this song into my creative lyrics and was humming while walking to my office after surveying the sky as it was a bright sunny Monday morning, and I was heading to my office solo since Rohan had some work, and he would make it a bit late to the office. Swati had already returned from Kerala trip a day ago,

and I was eager to meet her after a long full week. I had a few text conversations with her on Instagram in the last few days, and that confirmed she was genuinely interested in me. My only desire was to take her on a coffee date as soon as possible. With brainstorming some strategies and plans in my mind for my next action, I made my way to the Agarwal café.

As soon as I reached to the Agarwal café, I was delighted to see Swati at the payment counter, that too in the morning. Her brother was supposed to handle the café in the morning, I was thinking to myself. Seeing her at the café attired in a stylish black Kurti brightened my mood. My feel-good hormones burst forth in my body, and so I also sprinted towards her …

She glanced at me hurrying towards her, and she leaned in to give me a slight eye-roll from a faraway angle, I glanced at her and went straight away to speak to her …

One masala chai please; I ordered, giving a warm smile.

Sure … she smiled. Rahul, bring forward one masala chai, she instructed Rahul to deliver a masala chai for me.

Hey, the sun has risen from the west today, I informed her, looking at the sky and the bright weather.

What do you mean by that?? The sun rises in the east and sets in the west, she did her very best to show off her common-sense, giving me a puzzled look.

I meant, you are here at your café in the morning rather than in the evening, I tried to explain my sarcasm to her.

You don't have the habit of using straightforward words, right? She looked into my eyes.

It comes natural to me. When I was born, astrologers predicted that I will have a great sense of humor, although I don't believe in these silly things, but still, I responded with a sarcasm-filled smile.

You don't have any sense nor humor, forget about sense of humor, she ripped apart my sarcasm with her killer expression.

I could not do anything but to bow my head downwards and show respect to her humor.

Meanwhile, Rahul gave me the masala chai, and it was my best chance to flirt with her even more rather than sitting at a table far away from her and glancing at her. I seized the opportunity and decided to flirt.

So your Kerala trip is over, and you are back to work, I asked her again, this time with a sense of curiosity.

Yeah, it was a lot of good fun out there, I just got back yesterday and my brother had to go to Kanpur today for some urgent work, and now I have to work at the café whole day. He will be back in a couple of days time, until then, I have to take care of the café …

Boost in sales for the next 7 days, I responded to her, taking a big sip of my chai.

And why are you saying that, she pondered, making a pretty facial expression with her narrowed eyes.

You are still unaware of the USP of Agarwal café, I responded.

And What's that USP, she giggled this time. It looked like she was really liking my flirting skills, and I was loving it too.

It's you yourself, you have still not realized, plenty of guys have gathered here not to taste chai but to stare at your adorable face, I was tempted to respond to her but instead chose to keep my mouth shut for a few minutes.

While carrying on a conversation with Swati, I was sipping tea so slowly that it had gone cold, and I was no longer able to sip it more. I also cannot throw it since it may hurt Swati's ego. She was still intently staring at me, evaluating why I was not sipping the chai anymore. I gulped down the rest of the chai like a cold drink.

After gulping the chai like a cold drink, I flashed a facial expression that reminded me of a small child gulping homeopathic medicine, I drank, and it took me some time to wide open my eyes.

When I partially opened my eyes, I glimpsed Swati flashing me a cunning look from my blurry vision. The look was so dangerous that I thought I should just close my eyes and not let them open at all. I was ready to tell her sorry, but she had already figured out what I was going through and the reason for this awkward facial expression of mine.

Do you need one more tea, I think it has gone cold, am I right? She asked, gazing at me.

Yes, it was cold, but it was sweet, I said to her, intentionally bringing up the sweet word again.

She blushed. Rahul bring in one more masala tea, and it should be a double-hot tea, she suggested to him, but it sounded like she was teasing me again by adding double hot tea. She likes me, or she hates me, I thought to myself, with great confusion.

Don't worry, it's free, it's a replacement for the cold chai as you are our valued customer, she added with a smirking smile.

Yeah, I have more attendance to your café than I had in my entire engineering college, I am indeed a highly valued customer, I was trying to flirt with her again.

Stop it, it's not funny, Tripathi ji, she laughed and flaunted a lovely expression.

Tripathi ji sounded like pati ji to me, I was entrapped in my fantasy world. I did a small time travel, and it was my wedding day with Swati and varmala-ceremony was about to get under way. Before I could dream a bit more, I heard a voice, indeed a very soothing voice that came right into my ears and I woke up.

Tripathi ji, I think you are getting late, she raised her voice.

I flicked my eyes and I remembered I was dreaming. It was already 10 AM, and I was getting late for my office. I instantly flashed my iPhone X logo and scanned the QR code. It was unclear to me why she was still intently gazing at me while I was scanning the QR. I noticed that she was looking at my phone this time.

You know Tripathi ji, please don't take it other way, she wanted to say something.

I usually take it the other way, but I will not take yours, I assured her.

I think you have a great obsession with the iPhone Logo, she threw a bomb at me way before Diwali. However, she had a good laugh after that.

I took a moment to think, and I right away inserted my iPhone X inside my pocket. I pulled out my wallet and took some notes out.

No QR scan anymore, I am paying in cash from today, I responded to her with a low-key voice and a bitter facial expression.

She laughed again …

I picked up my bag and made my way straight to my office without a second's delay.

17

I am not feeling well yaar, please come back from the party, I informed Rohan on the call that I was suffering from fever. He responded, stating that he would be able to return to our room at about 9 PM. Rohan was attending a friend's birthday party, and he assured me that he would be returning soon. I sluggishly ascended the stairs and moved into my room with no energy left in my body. I was not at all feeling well, and I realized that I had a high fever, since I was shivering with cold and my head and neck were burning. I examined my head and neck with the back side of my Palm in a desi style to confirm whether I had a fever or not, and I surprisingly had a very high fever. I straight away picked my thermometer, and it showed 102 degrees Fahrenheit). I also didn't go to the Agarwal café that day because it got so late coming from the office and I had no strength left even to utter a word because of my fever. Even though I lost my taste buds, the fondness for chai can never wane in me. I can savour the chai even without my tongue. I was worried about what Swati would be speculating about me that I missed the café for the first time while she was present.

I switched from my office dress into casuals, and I wrapped myself in a warm blanket and snuggled on my bed with a pillow in my arms. I was hoping for Rohan to return as soon as possible. However, I felt that my fever was not dropping down; hence I decided to take medicine. I made my way to the kitchen and had some biscuits and snacks with so much discomfort, and I pulled out a paracetamol and swallowed it with water.

It was a little over 10 PM and Rohan had returned from the birthday party and was inquiring me about my health. My body temperature had declined a bit because of the medicine I had taken, and I informed Rohan that I was feeling well. I was still curled up on my bed with my blanket and Rohan showed me the party photos while he was laying on my bed. After exchanging some jokes and having some bizarre conversation, Rohan decided to go back to his room as he was feeling exhausted.

Aarav, please let me know if you would need any assistance from me, Rohan requested while exiting my room.

Sure, Rohan, I responded.

Just give me a call and I will be here, he promised.

Thanks, Rohan, I replied, and he headed to his room.

After he left the room, I wanted to sleep without wasting any further time, I turned off the lights and was about to go to sleep. It was a little after 11 PM, and I was still finding it difficult to sleep because I often used to sleep very late at night. I grabbed my phone and began listening to some songs. It was just after a few minutes, I received a notification, and it was a text-message from Swati on Instagram. I dived to Instagram, even with a very little energy to chat with her.

Hey Aarav, are you upset with me? She sent me a text-message.

Upset for what Swati, I texted back, and I was muddled too.

You did not show up to the café today, I felt like you were angry on my words which I had spoken to you in the morning regarding your phone, please don't take it other way, it was just a joke, she sent a text.

If you have felt bad, then I am sorry, she added.

Absolutely not Swati, I missed the café today because I got far too late coming back from my office and I also had been suffering from a high fever, I truly enjoy your great sense of humor, I responded with a smiley.

Thank god that you didn't take my words seriously; I was worried, she wrote.

For the very first time, I was able to know that Swati's soul was as pretty as she was, which made her appear so likable. She was a gem. I missed her café a single day, and she inquired whether there was something that made me feel uncomfortable. She couldn't even imagine how much do I like her, I thought to myself.

So sweet of you Swati, your IB = EB, I replied with a cheery emoji.

Now what's that, she inquired.

Your internal beauty is as wonderful as your external beauty, and actually, I am deeply sorry that I could not contribute in sales to your café today as a regular valued customer, I will make up for this tomorrow, I texted her.

Is shhh, she responded with a giggling emoji.

So You won't give up flirting even when you are sick, Right? Does it truly come natural to you? She asked.

It can be, sometimes astrologers can predict everything and it can be true, I responded

Why don't your hormones cool down when your body temperature is high? She threw a punch at me and I had nothing to defend myself.

I responded with a smiling emoji.

Fine, please take care of yourself and have some medicine if needed, she suggested.

For the first time, Swati and I were having such a smooth conversation between us. Now I was very convinced, she had actually given me a green signal. She asked me whether I was hurt or not, then inquired about my health, this was more than enough green signal from her. I was about to accelerate my next move now.

Common Tripathi, ask her for a date, be a real man, I was thinking to myself.

Swati, may I ask you something if you don't mind, I texted her.

Yes, please, she said.

Can we have coffee, day after Tomorrow together in the evening, I requested.

But you love chai Right, why would you have coffee together, she replied.

I mean, we can have chai as well but not at your café anywhere else, I wrote.

And why would you like to have chai with me together? Any specific reason for that, she inquired.

This was a reasonable question from her, I immensely used my brain. Actually, I am working on a project where the clients need some data of local successful business person so that the data can be used to help other businesses and I would need your help with this, I am new to my job, and it would send a great impression of mine to my leaders, I texted her.

So you will take my business data to help other business, right, She shot back.

I guessed more than her business model, she understood my business model of taking her on a coffee date. It's just some basic data like overall sales and growth per year, nothing major, I texted her back.

Don't you think you drive too fast, Aarav, she asked.

I knew this was her banger again. I tried to counter her with my humor.

There is absolutely nothing wrong in driving fast if there are no breakers, I am not violating the speed limit or breaking any rule, I countered her.

You are truly a very well-rounded engineer, she responded.

I responded with a giggle.

Now please let me know if we can join Swati, I pleaded with her again.

OK, I will think, she told me.

Please let me know when you will think, I asked her again.

After getting no response from her, I thought she might be thinking about the decision.

Are you thinking? I messaged her again.

Decision pending, she shot back.

I think my fever is rising, and I am not feeling well, please let me know your decision Swati, I intentionally tried to gain sympathy.

Ok, I will let you know the place and time. We can't go in the evening since I have to manage the café, I may be fine after 9 PM, but it should not be too late, only an hour and I have to get back before 10:30, is it OK? She asked.

More than OK, In fact, too OK, I replied to her in great amazement and flung my blanket in the air.....

18

"How much more time would you take Swati", I requested her to come as soon as possible while sending her a text message on Instagram. It was close to 9 PM, and I was waiting for her at Cirrus 9 all alone. Swati and I had mutually agreed to meet for a coffee at Cirrus9, the very same place where I along with Rohan and Kreepesh, visited earlier. I chose this place only because of its amazing beauty and its picturesque background that offered a great glimpse of the city. My only dream was to capture a selfie with Swati at this location, that would brighten up my day. However, she had not yet arrived and time was running out quickly. I ordered a shot of vodka in desperation and began sipping it. I had tried earlier to convince her to come with me together, but she denied, stating that she did not want to get caught red-handed with me. She had promised me a time that she would make it to the Cirrus9 at roughly about 8:45 PM sharp after taking care of her café, but she was half an hour late already. I attempted to send her a few more text-messages, but there was no response from her. I thought that she might be riding her scooty. My head was frustrated, and I wolfed down at least two glasses of vodka. I immediately started bombarding myself with plenty of questions such as, what if Swati does not turn up, my first date would go terribly wrong.

It was just after 9:30 PM, and I was giving up all my patience. Just after a few more minutes of exasperation, I leaned myself on my assigned chair and broadened my eyes and I could figure out Swati had just strolled into the restaurant. Trust me, I had never seen such a beautiful Girl ever before in mine whole life. As she stepped closer, I enlarged my eyes and I gazed at her from top to bottom. She was decked out in a luscious black color body-con, a black watch that paired well with her dress, a pair of high heel stilettos, and her long shimmering hair were flapping in the air. She had adorned herself with a bright red lip color and was carrying a black color small handbag in her left hand. She recognized me from a distance, and she ramped walked straight to me. As She approached closer, all the guys around started gawking at her, she jerked her head towards them and fluttered her silky hair in the air while exuding a lovely facial expression and lowered her eyebrows as if she indicated a direct-no to all the losers who were staring at her. I was wholeheartedly enveloped in her exquisite beauty. I gestured to her with a wave, and she strode to table no 9 where I was seated. I was still not sure whether I was dreaming or all this was for real. She came closer to me, and settled down on her seat, and I instinctively stood up to bid respect to her sublime beauty.

When she saw this behavior of mine, Swati cackled with laughter and even the waiters could not stop smiling at us, and I was there still standing respecting her sublime natural beauty.

Why do you always do this, Aarav? It's a public place, she remarked while glancing at the menu card.

Like what? I inquired.

Does these things come naturally to you or do you do it deliberately, she quizzed again.

It was instinctive, I have never seen someone as attractive as you since my date of birth, your beauty deserved to be respected, I responded.

She looked up while exuding a sweet facial expression and intently gazed at me.

Can you please sit now on your seat, Aarav, she made a request.

Sure, I settled into my seat.

Can I order something? She asked while tilting her eyes at the menu card.

Sure, Swati, I was quick to respond.

She called the waiter and ordered some snacks, and a cappuccino for both of us. However, she got furious because the table where we were seated was speckled with some dirt, and she asked the waiter to wipe that. The waiter promised to come back to wipe the table's surface, and then I grabbed my opportunity and pulled out my handkerchief and wiped the surface of the table for her and showed her how good a human being I was.

Waah tripathi ji, she clapped with her hands.

After 20 minutes, the waiter came back with our order and we both started having our cappuccino along with some snacks. We began sipping our first sip of the coffee, looking at each other in our eyes. I had already drank a glass of vodka before, and it was difficult for me to sip coffee because of the taste mixture, although I took it as an opportunity to flirt with her.

The coffee does not have any taste, right swati, the quality is so bad, I shared with her after having a sip.

It's good not that bad, she responded

Are you sure, I raised the question again

You are asking a café owner about liking the coffee of some other place? She shot back.

That's what I was saying, Agarwal café is the best café, I added.

Absolutely correct, she giggled.

It was my first coffee date with Swati, it was around half an hour that I had been hanging out with her and the clock displayed 9:45 PM. I could still not believe I was on a coffee date with her; however, she was not known to it as I had lied to her that I wanted some information about her café for one of my clients, and she clearly remembered that.

So you said you were looking for some info about my café for your client? What was that? She requested further information.

Yes, yes I remember, I responded.

Please ask as we are getting late now, she took a peek at her wristwatch.

Actually, the client that I was talking about has a business that specializes in offering business growth solutions to their clients; hence they are looking for some stats and data about successful business owners that might help them in giving their best solutions and services to their clients, I lied to her again.

And what is that data? She probed me.

Basic data such as What's your annual turnover of Agarwal café and what was the YOY rate of growth that you received over the years, I asked.

The annual turnover of Agarwal café is Rs 50 lakhs, and we have grown by 20 percent YOY over the years, she informed me.

Very impressive, I replied. I was blown away to know the annual turnover of her café, she was way more rich than I was expecting her to be.

She turned to look at her watch again to check the time.

I got it Swati, you are real rich, you don't need any iPhone, infact iPhone needs you, I jokingly told her.

Ohh Aarav this was not good from you, forget that joke na, I am so sorry for that, she pleaded this time displaying a simpatico expression.

I was completely in love with her, seeing her loving facial expressions that she made throughout all the time she had arrived.

When are you going back home for Diwali? She asked.

There is still three months left for Diwali, I will take the leave, I responded,

Yeah, I am very excited about this Diwali, I enjoy bursting crackers with my friends and family, she shared with me about her fondness for crackers.

I nodded

Would you be bursting crackers at your home, What kind of crackers you love, she asked with a curious face.

If I get a patakha like you in my life, why would I be even interested in another patakha and celebrating Diwali, I mumbled to myself.

Yes, Of Course Swati why not! I mean it's Diwali, we should enjoy it to the fullest, I responded to her after daydreaming about her for a few seconds.

Alright, Tripathi ji, I think we are getting late now, it is already more than 10 PM and I got to go home. Hopefully, you got all your answers that your client was looking for, she replied.

Nope, one more question is still left, I asked her.

And what's that?

Why don't you have a surname on your Instagram profile? I was very curious to know about this.

Because I don't want young guys to know my ID and send me follow request and try to connect with me, I am running a business and I don't want to ruin it, she explained the reasons.

I felt awkward, this was the exact thing that I have done which she did not want, I tried to distract her.

I called the waiter and asked him for the bill. Swati pressured me that she would pay the bill, but I won the negotiation and I paid the bill and also a nice tip to the waiter to convey a good impression of mine to her.

Alright, Swati I will accompany you to a certain distance and from there you can proceed without being caught red-handed, I told her.

She giggled, and we were all set to leave the café and just at that moment my mind interrupted as I had missed the chance to have a selfie with her. I can't leave without having a selfie with her, I have worked so hard to get her here with me, I reminded myself.

Can we have a selfie, Swati, please just for the sake of memory, I requested her.

Sure Aarav, take it, she smiled.

For that, I would require your brand-new iPhone for top-notch picture quality, I joked to her, but with a cheeky grin.

Oh god, Aarav, Please come out of that joke, she pleaded.

She pulled out her iPhone, and we posed for a wonderful selfie Together with the picture-perfect backdrop of Cirrus 9 bar and restaurant. Me with my celebrity would be the perfect caption for such pictures, I thought to myself.

Please send it on my WhatsApp, Swati, I requested her.

Why on WhatsApp? We are friends on Instagram right, I will send it there, she responded.

Actually, the Truth is, if you send it on Instagram, the picture's quality will get hindered, Please send me those pictures as a document file on What's App so that the quality is not tarnished, I explained this to her.

There is nothing like what you are saying, she shot back.

I am an engineer Swati and I know the algorithms, Why would I lie, I countered.

So shoot pictures again on your phone, she suggested.

Honestly, I have crashed my phone a few times and the sharpness of my camera is ruined, and I can't ruin your lovely face with my blurry camera, it would be a disrespect to your natural beauty, I responded but with a broken face, this time to gain some sympathy.

She peeked into my eyes for some time, and I lowered my head.

Alright, please give your number and I will send it once I get to my home, she responded.

We exchanged our numbers, and we made our way out of the bar and restaurant and I left her from a certain distance, and then she moved to her home.

.....

19

November 2018, Diwali

"The train has already arrived at the platform", one of the passers-by people informed me. It was close to 11:25 PM, and I was journeying back to my home after nearly six months. I was sprinting at the railway station, mainly because I was late. I was to board the Brahmaputra mail, whose scheduled arrival time at New Delhi Railway Station was 11:30 PM and was scheduled to reach Patna Junction at 2 PM on the next day. I was unable to reserve any other trains because of the festive rush, as Diwali was only two days left to celebrate. I could book the ticket only for this train in Tatkal Scheme, whose arrival time was slightly late at night. But the most amazing part was that I got my preferred seat of lower birth in the 2nd AC, and I was more than delighted about that. I was late because my cab turned up late, and I got confused whether I should book a new cab or go with the already confirmed cab whose driver was dreaming somewhere. This mix-up and driver's sloppiness got me late. The train was already halted at Platform No 1 and I desperately walked to get into my B2 Coach.

I stepped inside the coach and went straight to seat number B19, which was my assigned confirmed position. I laid my bag on the seat, chugged some water from my bottle and breathed a deep sigh of relief, and then leaned down and relaxed myself on the seat. After a few minutes, I picked up the loud sound of a train bell and the train began to speed up. Once the train accelerated, I instantly informed my mom that I had safely boarded the train.

I picked up the pillow and bedsheet, and then laid it on my seat, pulled the curtains and then stretched my body. I took my phone and checked out a few pictures of mine and Swati which we shot at Cirrus9 and that she had sent it through WhatsApp. I had her contact number, but we were still connected on chat since last three months. I had no strength still to directly call her number. However, we became so comfortable and close to each other in the past one month or so because of frequent chatting and interaction at her café daily. Although, I was still imagining of it as a dream that I went on a coffee date with her. I reminisced about each word that Swati spoke to me at Cirrus9. I vividly recalled her hot dress, her lovely eyes, her smoky lips and her most adoring expressions. There would be nobody as lucky guy as me in this whole world who would be blessed with such a patakha like her in their life, and that too on the occasion of Diwali, I thought to myself. After missing her so much, I exchanged a few chats with her and she replied Happy Journey. I tossed and turned the entire night on a rigid railway berth, as It was extremely difficult for me to sleep at the train berth. I watched a movie and I luckily fell asleep at around 4 AM.

It was 2:30 PM the next day and I arrived at the Patna Junction, a day before Diwali, and there seemed to be a lot of noise at the station. I probably speculated that it was because of Diwali, as people might be coming back to their home to celebrate this auspicious festival. I booked a bike and went straight to my home. After getting into my home at around 3:15 PM, I ate my lunch, spoke with my family members, shared my experience of my first ever corporate job and then disappeared to my bedroom since I was so exhausted and also did not have a decent sleep. I went to sleep at around 4 PM and then spent the rest of the day snoozing. I got up twice in between only to have a cup of chai and the second time was to have my dinner. I actually felt like I had become Kumbhkaran for a day, but I was still happy that I was not the Ravana. I hailed my creator "Shri krishna" who was also Shri Ram and who killed Ravana and went to sleep again.

It was the next morning at around 8 AM and It was Diwali. I got up and there was a lot of hubbub in and around my locality. People were embellishing their homes with LED lights, flowers, and other decorative items. I looked down and had a 360 view of the entire locality before I stepped down to the ground floor to have a sit-down with my family members. I finished my breakfast and our HOD, that is my father, brought in some new lights to brighten up our lovely 3-storey building. I had a niggling headache, so I requested my mom to give me a massage. I laid down on her lap and she was massaging my head, and we started having some discussions about Delhi and my job with each other.

How's the place, beta? mom asked while gently massaging my forehead.

It's okay mom, but there is a lot of rush, it appears like no one is interested in each other, they do work, earn money and get back to their home, that's it, I told her.

And how was your job experience at HCL, my mom wanted to know.

It's good mom, but it's also tiring at the same time, I responded.

I know beta, at the end of the day, it's a technical job, that's why I handed you packets of dry fruits that would take good care of your brain, she told me, and I raised my eyes towards her in disbelief.

Yeah, you understand it mom otherwise papa would just want me to work and work and do the naam Roshan kind of thing, I continued.

Shut up, he will hear you, mum asked me to tone down my voice.

What about your chaiwali, did you meet anyone ??she asked again, this time with a sense of curiosity.

Yeah mum there is a girl I like, I laughed while saying that.

Who is she, is she working in your same company, she was curious.

No mom, she is not working in my company, she is not present on the earth, she is not on the moon either but a moon herself, I laughed again.

Don't joke Aaru, Is she from our caste, she raised her eyebrows confused.

What mom, should I walk up to every girl I like and ask, hey are you from my caste, can I date you?? Can you share me your horoscope for matching, what's your rashi and gotra ?? Common mom, if I do this, I will probably get slapped by her, you all are still living in an ancient age, I got furious at my mom.

You are aware of your father very well, Aarav. We are brahmins, and he will never allow an inter-caste girl in our family, if he hears this, someone is from another caste, he will get angry, she said.

Alright, mom I am leaving now, I would rather not talk about this topic again and ruin my Diwali, mom please, I am only here for a few days for Diwali, let me have a great time, I pleaded her and walked away.

While I was on my way to my room. My father showed up again with some lights in his hands to decorate our entire house. Seeing this, my grandfather gave a nasty look. This was because he was the one who used to make payments for the electricity bill from his pension money, and he did not like the idea of so many light decorations. He believes that electricity should be protected. Seeing his expression, I also gave a devious smile, looking at my grandfather as if I were stating 'No excuse today'.

I have recently purchased some new lights aaru, some of the previous ones were not functioning, we have to decorate it today; otherwise we won't get time, my father requested me.

Alright, dad, it's already a little over 10 AM, and we should start decorating it all today, I agreed.

Everyone in our colony had already decorated their house, my father imparted to me the already reported news.

What about flowers dad, we don't have any flowers, I inquired.

Aah beta I forgot, can you pick up the bike and get in the flowers Right now Aarav, he gave the instruction.

I won't ride to the market with that bike, I will be borrowing a bike from some of my friends, I stated.

You fool, my bike is the best bike in the world, do you know it's mileage and how much money does it save on Petrol, I don't really know why this young generation is so obsessed with sports bikes which are in reality a nude bike, he came up with a verdict again.

Sorry dad, I would better not argue, I am going to bring the flowers right now, I told him.

What's the purpose of using so many lights, just to show off, my grandfather interrupted.

Because everyone is showing-off, and we should do it too. What everyone else is doing should be done by us, and it's a rule, I taunted and made sure that everyone listened to it clearly. I did this out of sheer frustration about inter-caste marriage.

Is his mood alright, why is he reacting in such a way, my father turned towards my mother who was standing near the gate of the room and asked her.

Everyone turned their eyes towards me and I left to bring the flowers.

I came back after an hour with the orange flowers for decoration and crackers for myself. We decked our entire home with lights and flowers with collective effort, and everyone, including me and my father, mother, and grandmother, appeared to be pleased and the only one that was unhappy was my grandfather, as usual. However, he got scolded by my grandmother when he was unwilling to show his happiness.

It was close to 7 PM and I turned my eyes from my terrace to our colony, the entire colony was festooned in lights and flowers. The city looked beautiful. I heard the sound of crackers bursting around and the kids frolicking in the streets. We finished our puja at around 7:30 PM, and then I had a few sweets, and we were all set to burst crackers. After blowing up a few crackers alone, I got bored, and I went to my friend's house and had some good time together while laughing at jokes and bursting crackers. I spent some time with them in a nearby park, and then it was almost 10 PM, and we had to head back to our respective houses.

I ate my dinner soon and set off to my bed. After I got to bed, and I was alone, so many memories and overthinking started popping into my head. I felt like I was missing something, I was not enjoying the day as much as I used to enjoy in previous years. Something was not Right and it was Swati. I was missing her and her words, her expressions. Her eyes were constantly glancing at me. I felt like she was close to me, and she was looking at me bursting crackers. I never had such feeling before for her, but I felt some different vibes and energy towards her when she was not closer to me. But I was also concerned about the discussion I had about inter-caste marriage in the morning with my mother. I was deeply in love with her and I could not be able to move away from her at any cost. I will sacrifice whatever it takes to get her into my life, I promised to myself before I fell asleep in her dreams.

20

May 2019

After nearly 6 months.

"You are deeply in love with her bro, when are you going to propose her", Rohan was curious. I am planning Rohan, Very shortly I will propose to her, I responded. It was exactly one year of working in HCL technologies, and I was promoted to C2 from C1 and was honoured with the distinguished performer award for the year, followed by a 10 percent salary hike in my annual package. Now my annual package was approx 11 lakhs from the initial 10 lakhs. I was very pleased that day, and I relayed this wonderful news to my parents immediately. My father was extremely proud of me that I was on the perfect path, and I was blossoming in my career. After Kreepesh left our flat, Rohan and I had managed to rent a flat soon after the previous tenants vacated it in a close vicinity. It's a 2 BHK flat and is decent enough; however, the rent is slightly higher, which Rohan hesitates to pay, taunting me that his annual package is below me. The absolute best part of this newly rented flat is that it's only 500 metres walking distance to Agarwal café, and it's located in Raipur Khadar itself, where we stayed for almost a year. However, the surrounding areas are not as great as the previous flat, but we have made compromises on all of it. We are still very close friends with Kreepesh, and we often meet each other at our flats and spend some lovely time together.

During this one year of my living in Delhi, I managed to only have Instagram and What's app conversations with Swati along with some rare voice calls, and we went on some unofficial coffee dates, but I have not proposed to her until date. She knew that I liked her, we have found ourselves very comfortable talking to each other and exchanging text messages. In fact, she shares me everything, even the smallest of things that happens in her entire day, just the way a girlfriend does, and I respond to her every message while working in my office. We both share about all our hobbies, likes, family, past and present with each other while being emotionally attached to each other, and we know every little detail about each other's personalities. She has not confessed that she likes me, nor do I, but we engage in conversation for hours and hours daily. I certainly could not stay happier the entire day if I didn't see her text message. She was my favourite habit. We never fail to talk and laugh at our sense of humour at the Agarwal café in the evening. She never misses her evening presence at the café. After discussing with Rohan, I decided that it was the most suitable time for me to inform her about my promotion and also propose to her and make her my girlfriend. I guessed she might be eagerly waiting for me to confess to her about my love and I should not delay it, rather propose to her as soon as possible.

It was just after 7 PM, as usual, and I was coming back from my office alone as Rohan was not there with me. Rohan already knew that I will have some interaction with Swati at the café; hence he had chosen to stay with me in the morning only and not in the evening to allow my relationship to progress without any roadblock. In the morning, he could joke around with Abhay, who had become one of his great friends over the time, he was Swati's brother. He further allowed me to communicate freely with Swati in the evening by not accompanying me. I was exhausted that day and I strolled straight to the Agarwal café and ordered for a cup of adrak chai. I instructed Rahul, the teenage boy, to pass on my message to the tea maker to add some extra adrak to the chai.

What happened Tripathi ji, extra adrak today, Swati pondered as she gazed at me.

I have a bit of headache today, so I would like to have some extra adrak in my chai, I looked at her worn-out and took a deep breath.

Are you okay? A lot of work and stress might be the reason I guess, Swati pointed out, looking at me exhausted.

Yes Swati, I am completely fatigued today, and also I am not feeling well, I informed her.

Are you nazuk kali, 'are you a delicate bud', she cracked a smile while jabbing at my manliness.

I am not in a mood to joke today, I responded.

So what mood are you in? She examined me, looking straight into my eyes.

There is good news to share, I told her while distracting her from her flirtatious topic.

And what's that good news? She asked in curiosity.

I have just been promoted to C2 from C1 in HCL with a 10 percent salary hike, this is my first-ever promotion in my corporate job, I am really thrilled about this, I responded in a very ebullient tone.

Many congratulations Aarav, you certainly deserve that, She expressed her happiness.

Thanks, Swati.

I could see her being extremely pleased about my success. It seemed like it was her success. I sensed it from her body language. She was genuinely filled with joy and she showed it. Meanwhile, Rahul handed me my special adrak chai and I immediately started sipping it. I was having my adrak chai in my hand and my headache was relived to some extent. I thought to myself, let's have some banter now ...

Tripathi ji, where is your promotion party, she interrupted and continued to stare at me.

It's on the way Swati, something special is planned for you, I responded in a flirty way.

Why only for me, why not your friends, am I a special one, she questioned while narrowing her eyebrows.

You are special indeed, I responded.

And why? She asked with a lovely expression on her face.

Can we have a cup of sweetest chai together, Swati, I indirectly asked her for a coffee date while not responding to her flirtatious question.

What do you mean by sweetest, chai is always sweet, she said. She was aware that I was asking her for a date, but she preferred to promote her over acting skills, which I did not like, I decided to ask her directly.

Can we go on a coffee together? I asked again, looking into her eyes.

No way Aarav, I have a lot of work to handle, she over acted again.

Can we go? I raised the question again.

You are getting late Tripathi ji, she responded with a giggle, she was thoroughly enjoying it.

Can we go? I asked her again, peering into her eyes.

Shhh okk I will let you know Tomorrow, you are a terrible actor for sure, she praised my acting skills.

I love over acting, I sarcastically praised her over acting skills to which she could not stop herself from bursting into laughter.

And who is that actress whose acting you love, she was in full mood and was aggressively flirting with me continuously.

Someone whose expressions are more important than Java and whom I love to code more than python, I tried my best to show my technical skills and the reason as to why I was promoted.

Don't be an engineer all the time Aarav, I don't understand these points, she responded.

Please let me know by Tomorrow ma'am, everything will be cleared soon, I shall be eagerly waiting for your message, I told her.

I pulled out my wallet and paid in cash in front of Swati.

And yes, I am going to buy the latest version of iPhone 11 soon and then only I will pay via UPI, I taunted.

Please get lost from here, she indirectly abused me and I made my way back to my flat.

This was one of the most satisfying days for me. I was promoted, I got a hike in salary, and now I was taking Swati on an official date and I would propose to her. We had grown very close to each other in this one year, and I was very sure that she would accept my proposal. I lost my appetite because of exuberance and over eagerness and could not eat anything that night. I spent the whole night dreaming about how I would propose to her. I viewed several videos of learning how to propose and also tried several proposal position.

21

Sure, please confirm it for this Sunday from 7 PM, I informed the manager on call and I booked the Ottino at West View of the ITC Maurya online. With its rustic stone walls, molded iron chandeliers, well-stacked books and wall plates, the interior of this Italian restaurant seemed very aesthetically pleasing. The stupendous outdoor section, with a water body, stage, bar and incredible views of the verdant Delhi ridge, that set this fine-dining restaurant apart from the rest. The menu is filled with traditional Italian dishes including antipasti, live grills, wood-fired pizzas and pastas. The Sunday brunch with live music was extremely popular. The open sky and live performances made this restaurant ideal for date night or an evening out with close ones. I thought this place might be the best to propose Swati. However, this location was at 20 KM away distance from sector 126, Noida and I still chose it because I wanted to book a place at a far away location so that nobody would catch us together.

It was just after 7 PM and Swati was on right time. I had already taken my place and was anxiously waiting for her. She walked into the Ottino wearing a black colour one piece, that was snugly fitted to her body and it flaunted her hour-glass figure. I lifted my eyes towards her, and she stepped forward. She was offering a classy stare to all the other guys who were intently looking at her. She had tucked her long glimmering hair behind her ear, and she looked absolutely gorgeous. She had put on a beautiful pair of white earrings that perfectly complemented her beauty. Her eyes were encircled with dark kajal, and she slathered on a light red lip colour to her luscious lips that was enough to blow off my mind. She strolled forward like a queen of the kingdom with her pair of high heels stilettos, and I widened my eyes. She was a true masterpiece of natural beauty.

Meanwhile, she settled into her seat in front of me, and I was still staring at her, I was entirely wrapped up in her." Are you there, Aarav?" she interrupted, Yes, Swati, I instantly woke up from my daydreaming. What would you like to order? I asked her. She picked up the menu card and started having a look at the menu to order something for both of us. I was all the time intently staring at her, and I was a little anxious too. I was planning to propose to her in a bit of time and I really did not know how would she react? I was very hopeful that she would accept my proposal, but also worried, thinking about what if she does not accept my proposal." This place looks beautiful, Aarav, she commented while rolling her eyes over the Ottino at the West View." A place that you would remember for years, I mumbled." Did you say something, she pondered while exuding her adorable smile? She was killing me from her expressions. I already had a set plan to propose to her, and I thought it was the best time to execute the plan …

I signalled to my already prearranged manager with a wave to bring a cup of coffee for me and her. He drooped his eyebrows and blinked his eyes. Swati and I were having some conversations and shortly after 15 minutes, two cups of coffee were delivered by the waiter, and a red love heart was printed on both the cups of coffee, the waiter handed to us the coffee and went straight away without uttering a single word. Swati was a bit taken aback as she looked at the love heart painted on the cup.

When did you order this coffee Aarav, and why is there a love heart printed on the cups, Swati looked befuddled as she was still unsure about what to order and this order was delivered from nowhere. She instantly rolled her eyes all over and turned back to other tables to confirm if they also had that love heart painted on the cups.

As soon as she turned back towards me, I was already down on my knees holding a beautiful ring in my right hand and I was proposing Swati.

Oh God, she clasped her hands on her mouth and her words were more than a whisper. She stood up instinctively from her seat." Aarav, what are you doing, everyone is watching us", she said while tilting her head at everyone around. Meanwhile, everyone around us shifted their eyes towards her to wait for the decision of Swati which was still pending.

"Swati, from the moment I have met you, you've been the cream to my coffee, the soul to my life, the semicolon to my code" I said, my voice was trembling with emotion.

Swati widened her eyes as she looked at my romantic gesture. What are you saying Aarav?, she responded.

You know, Swati, I like you more than Java and Python. Your café is the best memory location where you are the best variable that remains constant in my heart. Whenever I try to code your natural beauty to my heart, my heart throws a compilation error, which gets really difficult to handle. You are an exception Swati and I love exception handling, I proposed to her in my coding language.

What are you speaking Aarav, she was nervous, and her voice was shaking.

I love you Swati, will you be mine girlfriend, I raised the ring towards her.

She could not hold back her tears from flowing out of her eyes. She held the beautiful ring in her hand and lifted me up. She kissed the ring and hugged me wholeheartedly. I lifted her in the air and swirled her around. I will be your girlfriend, Aarav, she whispered in my ears and kissed my cheeks. I could not contain my emotions and they spilled from my eyes as happy tears. I kissed her lips, and we could hear so many claps and cheers around from the people. Decision pending was changed to Yes. The manager right away brought in a mouth-watering cake with a written text" Aarav loves Swati" and was placed on our table. I never knew I was such a good director that I could even direct blockbuster movies. Everything was going in as planned, I saw Swati so much cheerful for the first time in my life. She was behaving like a small, happy child.

We sliced the cake with so much love and also passed along the pieces of cake to the manager and the waiters around. I licked the fingers of Swati while she served me the sweetest cake with her delicate hands. Soon, The lights of the restaurant changed to red and pink mainly because it was the bar time and as soon as it went all dark for a few seconds. Swati came closer to me and I held her waist and grabbed her towards me." The slow background music started playing, *'Naino ki chaal hai, makhmali haal hai, Neechi palkon se badle samaa, Rab ki nemat hai teri nigaahein, Jisme basti hai uski duayein, Aise naino ki baaton, mein koi kyun na aaye, tere naina tere naina'*, I looked into her eyes.

I love you Swati, I love you so much, I spoke very close to her lips.

I love you too Aarav, I have been waiting for this day for so long, thanks for making this day a wonderful memory Aarav, she said in a jubilant tone.

I kissed her on her forehead, you know what you taste very sweet, I flirtatiously told Swati.

Stop it, Tripathi, she slapped me straight on my face.

Tripathi ji was changed to only Tripathi now …

After our slow break-dance for around 15 minutes, We plopped back on our seats and I could not believe that I had just proposed Swati and my proposal was accepted. The glow of joy could easily be glimpsed in my eyes and Swati's eyes too. We were both excited, and soon we decided to order something for us as we had not eaten anything in exuberance and also we would get late. Swati picked up the menu card, and she ordered food for both of us.

I gestured the waiter to bring in the order quickly as time was slipping by quickly and Swati would get late for her home.

We enjoyed some veg recipes, and we got carried away with our banter again.

Why are you staring at me so much today, Aarav? Haven't you seen me before, Swati pointed out while chomping on a small portion of her food.

I have seen you as Swati before, who owns the Agarwal café. Today, I am staring at you as my girlfriend who owns my heart, I responded.

I am only yours right, Swati burst into laughter as she displayed a lovely facial expression.

You are **ONLY MINE**, I reminded her.

Swati blushed, and I flaunted my glistening white teeth too.

We were engrossed in each other's love so much that we did not even realize that It was already around 10 PM and time ticked by very rapidly. Swati and I also had a cup of vodka on my special request, and she accepted and drank it all. I could not believe that she did not even vomit. She was such an all-rounder. We were about to leave since she had to go home as soon as possible. I paid the bill quickly, and we were greeted, *come again sir*, by the receptionist and we left …

We were so engaged talking to each other that we barely looked at our watch or our phone. It was 11 PM and she was late. We could not find anyone on the side roads where we were having a conversation with each other. However, main roads always have traffic and are busy.

Can I drop you, Swati? It's too late now, I told her.

I will go Aarav, I don't want anyone to come across me with you, my brother would be informed.

Common Swati it's already late night and who is bothered to see you at this time, we are wearing helmets Right, it should not be an issue, I assured her.

Swati gestured no with her hands.

I am dropping you and that's final, no argument please, I added.

Ohhk alright I will ride, Swati agreed.

Please ride slow Swati, I requested her as I had no trust in her driving skills.

And why? She wanted to know.

I want to make these memories as beautiful as I can, this day won't come back again, and I would like to spend as much time as possible With you, I explained.

You know what Aarav, you are such a dumb guy, she raised her voice.

I was so baffled as to why she called me dumb all of a sudden. Why? What happened, Swati, I responded.

You are the dumbest guy, I am your girlfriend now, and I am alone, nobody is watching us, she told me, grabbing my waist towards her.

As soon as she said this, I grabbed her waist and kissed her intensely. I caressed her hair with my fingers and smooched her, she stroked my lips, touching my neck. I love you, Swati, I kissed her again. She clutched my neck and started kissing me. I was immersed in her love, my hormones surrendered to her. It was as if I didn't wish for anything in this world apart from Swati. She hugged me more for about 5 minutes, and it was over. My eyes were still closed. As soon as I opened my eyes slowly, Swati was standing right in front of me, laughing at me.

Pinch me Swati, am I dreaming, did you just kiss me? I asked.

Should I kiss you again? Swati pinched me so hard that I winced in pain.

I rubbed my heart again, thank you, Swati, thank you for accepting this poor guy as your boyfriend, I taunted her funnily.

I am getting late now Aarav, I love you, Please take these keys and ride fast, I have to make it to my home as quickly as possible, she handed me the keys of her scooty.

We fitted the helmets and I started driving the scooty at around 60 km per hour. She gripped my waist from behind with her hands and rested on my shoulders. She was so in love with me, it felt like she was in a relationship with me for so long. I was able to feel her affection towards me. I could do anything to get her in my life, anything, I mumbled to myself.

More 2 km is left Swati, should I go now, I informed her. We were about to reach sector 47.

Swati got down from the scooty and took the front seat.

Yes Aaru, I will leave now, text me once you reach your flat alright, don't forget, she requested.

You know what Swati call me baby now, I am not Aaru, Tripathi or Tripathi ji, I am baby, get that in your mind OK, I was staring at her.

OK, baby, she blushed and accelerated her scooty. I made my way to my flat.

.....

22

August 2019

After nearly 3 months.

"Are we heading to Manali or not? Please rectify this Swati, I was furious at her over the phone call as she was reluctant to go on a Manali trip with me.

I was already in a 3-month relationship with her which was chock-full of happiness, sweet moments and squeals of delight. I spent long hours on my phone chatting with her even in my office hours. Furthermore, I was still living with Rohan in our two BHK flat in Raipur Khadar and there were no complications at all. Apart from that, Rohan and I frequently met Kreepesh and everything was going really well. However, I was entirely absorbed in Swati's love. It felt like I had known her for years. I found myself caring a lot for her. My love for her was expanding day by day. There was barely an hour when I could stay without chatting with her. I used to get annoyed if I won't talk to her even for a few hours. I was in love with Swati, a love that had no bounds and was 100% pure. I used to visit her Agarwal café regularly and also used to spend some time with her for about 10 minutes loitering on the streets before I went back to my flat. That was my new daily routine in the evening. Swati and I were becoming very close to each other. Even when I was in my office catching up on projects, I would look at her last seen every now and again to know whether she was online or offline. I would be waiting for her messages. I was neither focused on my work nor worried about that. My heart and soul only prayed for Swati in my life. We used to text each other while I was in my office at frequent intervals, and I would not miss spending time with her at Agarwal café in the evening.

During the three months of our relationship, Swati has been very kind towards me. She cared for me as much as I cared for her. She was a beautiful soul. She loved and cared for me like my mother used to do. It seemed like we were made for each other. We got so comfy that it never looked like we were strangers at some point of time. She once told me that whenever I had got close to her since the very first day she saw me, she felt a different energy, an energy that she never felt before speaking to anybody else. It was like our souls were clamouring for each other to connect. We were the heart and soul of each other.

I decided to convince Swati to go on a Manali trip with me, since we hardly had time to spend with each other alone apart from the evening meet at the café. However, she denied, saying that she cannot lie to her family and what if her brother gets informed. She wanted to be on the safer side. We used to talk in the evening, but I aspired for Swati to be beside me for the entire day, not entire day but for the entire week so that I can share my feeling with her. I wanted to love her, care for her and give her all the love that she deserved.

It was Monday at exactly 7 PM, and I was on my way back from my office. I had a serious argument with Swati on the phone call earlier that morning regarding the Manali trip. I was not at all happy that she denied going on the trip with me. I was hoping to take her on the trip, and I will take her on the trip, I thought to myself. I made my way to the Agarwal café, where Swati was busy collecting the bill amount of the customers.

One adrak chai please, I requested.

Sure sir, Swati gestured Rahul to bring me an adrak chai.

I was not pleased with her that day, but I loved her, and all my anger turned into joy as soon as I glanced at her. She was looking red-hot. She was dressed in a red colour kurti, and she teamed it with a pair of big elliptical white ear earrings in conjunction with her rectangular modern specs, and she had styled a hair bun on the back. She was looking cute in spectacles. Every so often, I felt Like my horoscope was so blessed to have a girl like Swati as my girlfriend…

Don't stare at me Aarav, have you not Seen me before, she peeked into my eyes.

You know what Swati, this kalyug is not for you, you are made for Satyug, you are not a mere human being, but a queen, and you should not sit on this normal chair but a throne, I said this line looking at all the other guys who were gawking at her from a far distance.

Is Shh, What a filmy line, she laughed her heart out. She cracked up so loud, that all the other people around us started staring at us.

Aarav, please don't do this, it's a public place and what if someone informs my brother about this, please don't flirt here, she added while tilting her head towards everyone.

Then where should I flirt, do we spend time alone, Swati? You know that I love you a lot, but where should I show my love and care for you, on What's App and Instagram? I said in a stern tone.

I agree with that Aarav, but how can I go alone with you telling lies to my family? What if my family members get informed. Everything will be screwed up, please think about it Aarav.

Alright then, better you categorize our relationship as an online relationship or a part-time relationship, that's all I can say, I was offended.

It's not like that Aarav, please understand, give me some time to think, I will figure out some way, she did her best to calm down my anger.

I want to spend some time with you alone Swati, not in a bar or café but somewhere else where there is only you and me, I responded.

In Manali right? She asked, looking at my bright red, angered face.

She was already aware about the Manali trip as we had a long argument on the phone call about the Manali trip early that morning, and she was still asking about Manali as if she didn't know anything. It felt like she was taking a dig at me. I decided not to say a word to her, and I sipped my tea.

A beautiful young attractive girl will go on a Manali trip with a young guy who also likes to flirt a lot and that too alone, Swati added.

I still did not respond to her as she was in a full mood to flirt with me and I knew that. By doing this, she was not calming me down, rather making me more angry at her.

What if you take my advantage, Aarav? She asked again.

She was getting me more angry.

Tripathi ji drives so fast, he wants to drive on the highway now, she added a sarcastic comment.

Alright, Swati, I am not going to say anything now, do whatever feels right for you, I finally responded to her.

Ohhh, are you angry at me Aarav, she asked in a very sweet tone.

I am not angry, I am just sad, I responded with a deplorable face.

I will think about it Aarav, I will let you know. You know that my family members will not allow this. I have to make a proper plan with Ridhi to go on a trip with you. Please Understand Aarav.

I would rather not understand anything Swati, we are going on a Manali trip, and you make the planning whatever you want to make. I can wait, but I will go, and that's final. Take Ridhi with you, that's fine, but we are going, I said in a serious tone.

I took out cash from my wallet and paid it to the café.

Pay it using your new iPhone Aarav, she tried to cool me down, but I was angry.

Please don't joke Swati, I'm not in that mood right now, I told her.

I was unhappy, and I went straight to my flat without uttering a single word.

23

Is this true Swati, can you please confirm? I spoke to her on the phone call, brimming with excitement." Yes, Aarav, we are heading to Manali next Sunday, she responded. This is the very best news, Swati, I will apply for office leave and book the tickets today itself, I said." Book one additional ticket for Ridhi, she will be travelling with us, she informed me on the call." Are you taking Ridhi on the trip, I inquired." Yes Aarav, without her, I will not be permitted to go anywhere on the trip, my family members know her very well and her family too, and they trust her, I lied to my parents that I am going to Manali with Ridhi and a couple of other college friends, she explained the plan." No worries baby, I am glad that we are going on the trip, I will compromise on everything, I smiled and disconnected the call.

So, eventually, we were making our way to Manali. The excitement was the same, as hitting a first ball for six. I was very overjoyed to hear this wonderful breaking news. She had made a masterful plan to convince her parents for the Manali trip. Together, she and her friend Ridhi made this plan and for the first time in my life, I liked Ridhi not because of her appearance, but she helped us with our plan to go on a trip to Manali. I should be grateful for that. I quickly left an email to my Manager for a 5-day leave from next Sunday, and I began looking for tickets. That day was Friday and I had 10 days still left for the trip. I decided to book train tickets instead of a flight because Chandigarh was close to Delhi, and it would take only 50 minutes to make it to Chandigarh from New Delhi via air, which I did not intend to do. My goal was to spend as much of the time with Swati and make this trip an unforgettable one. I chose to travel by train to Chandigarh and then go via a bus to Manali. The other reason for not booking a flight ticket was that if I get caught by someone with Swati, I can jump off the train, but I cannot jump from the aeroplane. I began searching for train tickets, but most of the tickets were sold out. I at long last stumbled upon AGC HSX EXP (11905) whose arrival time was 10 PM, and it would reach us at Chandigarh station at 3:30 AM. Roughly it was a 5-hour journey, which I preferred as I would get much more time to chat with Swati. I booked the second AC ticket and the reason for that was we all together were 3 people and 1st Ac has 4 seats or either 2 seats that means one stranger will be sharing the cabin if we get into the 4 seat cabin and Ridhi will miss out if I book a 2 seat cabin that is a coupe and I did not enjoy the idea of displeasing Ridhi; hence I reserved tickets in the Second Ac, which was one side lower berth for myself, one side upper birth for Swati just above my head so that we can sit and talk at the lower birth and one upper berth for Ridhi Ahuja.

The next Sunday

It was close to 9:30 PM and I, Swati along with Ridhi, reached the New Delhi railway station on time. Our train AGC HSX EXP was at around 10 PM. Ridhi was accompanying us on the trip as planned. I did find it a bit awkward while talking to Swati while Ridhi was right next to us, but there was no other way to take Swati on a trip alone. Swati had promised Ridhi that she would not feel bored, and we both would take good care of her. Ridhi was actually a good girl as I did not know much about her since

I had no interaction with her in the past, but she had that habit of doing her own taarif which I hated a lot. However, I only required her support and nothing else, which she did with pleasure. The train arrived on time, and we boarded the train and the train began to accelerate.

After having some conversation for an hour with both Swati and Ridhi, it was shortly after 11 PM, and Ridhi informed Swati that she was feeling drowsy as she had not slept well in the previous night. We planned to rest on our respective berths. There was still 4 hours left to reach our destination. I could not flirt with my celebrity Swati since Ridhi was there, it felt a little odd for me and Swati did understand that why I was so silent. She was intently gazing at me and passing a grin. I was patiently waiting for the right moment to have a proper banter with her, and I was confident she would not be able to counter me this time. It was nearly 11:30 PM and as a good responsible human being, I decided to lay the bedsheets for Swati at her side upper sleeping berth. I spread her bedsheet first and then placed the pillow, and then I did the same for mine.

You can get some rest now Swati, I requested her to sleep or either rest after setting the bedsheets on her birth.

She nodded.

She pulled her shoes off which I kicked it inside the side lower birth to make sure that her shoes are not lost or stolen by anyone while we are sleeping. At the end of the day, I was a desi guy and I had lost so many slippers and shoes in my past or were stolen by someone.

I can't imagine Swati walking barefoot at the Chandigarh railway station and all the people strolling by staring at her, this thought terrorized me.

Although, Ridhi was looking a bit disappointed after witnessing all my love and care for Swati. She was feeling alone, I guessed. Swati gestured me from the side upper birth to spread her bedsheets too so that she does not feel uncomfortable. Swati gave me a green signal; hence it was not much of a worrying sign for me.

Let me lay down the bedsheets for you, I am taller, I will do that for you, I said to Ridhi after getting a signal from Swati as Ridhi's berth was an upper berth, and she was struggling to spread her bedsheets; hence I offered to do it for her.

No Aarav I will do it, it's not an issue for me, she responded.

Let him do Ridhi, Swati raised her voice and made a request to her.

I laid Ridhi's bedsheets on the upper berth and gave her a pillow before I requested her to rest on her berth. Ridhi herself pulled her sandals off and got it hidden somewhere inside the lower birth between some trolleys of other passengers. She was smart.

I settled into my seat which was side lower berth and I looked at Swati by elevating my eyes to the side upper berth which was just above my head and I did that almost whole night since I had a problem of falling asleep in railways births, so I utilized my nighttime listening to songs and staring at my beautiful celebrity. She looked beautiful, even when she was sleeping. I believed god had taken some extra time to code Swati, although she was not a software.

24

Hey Swati, please hurry, we have arrived at the Chandigarh Railway Station. I informed her upon reaching our destination, who was dozing like a Kumbhkaran. We arrived at Chandigarh station at around 5 AM and the train was half an hour late. She rushed to get up and climbed down from her side upper berth. I spoke to Ridhi, and we picked up our bags and made our way out of the railway coach. Swati was still drowsy and hence she asked for her favourite adrak chai. I had already booked our bus tickets. The HRTC bus was at around 6 AM, and it would reach us to Manali within 5 hours. I, Swati and Ridhi had a couple of biscuits and chai at the railway platform so that we didn't feel drowsy, and then we set off quickly to the bus stand.

We boarded the bus a few minutes before its scheduled departure time, and we took our reserved seats. Swati settled into the window seat and I sat right next to her, while Ridhi was seated in front of us. I felt really bad for Ridhi. The bus speeded, and we were on the way to Manali. It came off like a dream to me, Swati was with me, and we were en route to Manali, something that I had never imagined being possible. She plugged in her AirPods and started listening to songs. I did the same. Swati leaned out of the window to admire the enchanting scenery along the way to Manali, while I was staring at my beautiful scenery, which was Swati herself. For half an hour I was so lost in her that I did not utter a word.

After another two hours, the bus driver hit the brakes near a *dhaba* to allow the passengers to have their breakfast if they wanted to, since the bus departure time was very early in the morning. All of us sprinted towards the dhaba since we were hungry. We all three had 'kachori sabzi' at the dhaba and trust me, the taste was so mouthwatering. My girlfriend asked for tea again, and I fulfilled her demand straight away. After a few more hours of our journey and a lovely window view, we finally made it to Manali at around 11 AM. I had booked the Montana Blues Resort via booking.com and the check in time was 12 PM. We showed up at the resort half an hour before the check in time.

I had booked two rooms via booking.com, can you please confirm, I reached out to the Front desk staff at the hotel.

The staff rolled his eyes and started staring at us, I realized he was looking at one guy and two girls, which made me feel very, very awkward. Swati issued me a life-threatening grimace.

I have booked two rooms, please confirm that. I spoke two rooms with a lot more effort and a raised voice to blow away all his fantasy conundrums.

One for me and one for my friends, I continued, after getting no response from him. If I had been alone, I would have abused that fantasy loving guy and kicked him.

He finally responded, yes sir, Please give me a few seconds. I can confirm your booking, he added, but the check in time is around 12 PM, we are working on getting your room ready, please wait for half an hour in the cafeteria.

OK, please do it quickly as we are knackered, I responded.

Please provide me your Aadhaar card, sir, he requested.

I pulled out my Aadhaar card from my wallet and handed it to him for the check. He scanned the Aadhaar card and passed it back to me. He did the same for Swati and Ridhi.

Thank you sir, please make the payment, and I am working on getting your room ready as soon as possible.

Sure, I paid the booking payment, and we headed straight to the cafeteria to spend the remaining time.

We checked in inside the hotel room at around 12 PM. However, the guys' expression was still imprinted in my mind. He was a bastard.

The rooms allotted were 309 and 310 on the third floor. Ridhi checked in to her room, which was 310, and I and

Swati checked in to the other room, which was 309. I inserted the card and opened the gate of our room. Swati switched on the lights. I locked the door from inside and Swati stood in front of me while resting her hands on her waist. I was staring at her, she looked at me.

Are you happy now? You won. She asked while maintaining a lovely facial expression.

I will be happy on the day when I win you, Swati, I responded.

We both glimpsed into our eyes.

There was some sort of eye contact that was going on between us. This was the first time we were alone. It took us so much of planning and execution to get there. We laughed, and I pulled Swati from her waist and kissed her, she hugged me. I held her hands, and we sat together on the bed, she kissed my forehead. Just as I wondered how good a human being, Swati is, she grabbed my collar and kissed me like a wild animal.

How are you feeling, Aarav? She asked, looking into my eyes. She was probably happier than me.

Something that I can't explain right now, I told her.

Please explain, she asked again.

I will explain, but for now, please allow me to have a nap as I am exhausted, and I did not fall asleep like kumbhkaran on a train berth, I said.

Can you please answer whom are you referring to Kumbhkaran here?, she raised her eyebrows.

I said in general, like kumbhkaran sleeps a lot, I hope you are familiar with that, I answered with a cheeky smile.

I am aware of everything, don't you ever consider me to be a fool, she reminded me.

After having a banter with her, we took showers, and we decided to have a nap. We took a two-hour nap and

I cuddled her while sleeping. After we got up, it was around 2:30 PM. We decided to order our lunch from the hotel. I called in Ridhi, and we all had our lunch together. However, we made sure that none of the staff members would keep an eye on us entering and moving out of our rooms, as the two rooms were booked for me and the other for Swati and Ridhi. However, Swati and I were staying in the same room, and we were very cautious. This was just a precautionary measure from us just not to make a scene, we could easily see other unmarried couples too, staying in the hotel. That gave us a lot of confidence.

We did not walk out that day for the whole day. We ordered snacks and tea in the evening, and we chatted a lot. I opened up about my feelings with Swati which I always wanted to share, and she shared her love for me, too. I also called Ridhi inside our room regularly, as she might get bored sitting all alone in her room. We made sure she did not get bored and thoroughly enjoyed the trip as much as we were doing.

Soon it turned 9 PM and Swati decided to take her shower again. When I questioned her why, she takes a shower twice in a day. She offered an explanation by saying that it's her daily routine as she manages the Agarwal café in the evening. As soon as she returns home from the café, she takes a shower and then eats her dinner and then goes to bed. This was unfathomably new to me.

Not everyone is like you, who does not like having a bath, she taunted me while getting inside the bathroom.

I don't know what problem you have with me, I raised my voice.

I plopped on the couch that was inside our hotel room and started scrolling my social media. After about 20 minutes, Swati stepped out after finishing her shower.

I don't know who takes that long to take a shower, I do it within 2 minutes, I thought to myself. She was wearing a white gown to her knee-length, and she stood in front of the mirror while looking into the mirror. She reached for a towel and started drying her dripping wet hair. She was looking astoundingly beautiful, which encouraged me to stand up from my couch and rush towards her. I moved closer to her and stood right behind her without notifying her. She sensed me standing behind her, and she flicked her long hair towards my face, her wet hair sprayed drips of water on my face. I was so immersed in her that those tiny water drips of her wet hair smelled like a God-given perfume to me. I suddenly came back to my senses and I saw her looking into my eyes. I grabbed her waist and pulled her towards me. She hesitated, and before she could utter any word with her beautiful satin-smooth lips, I kissed her.

I love you Swati, I don't understand why, but I feel so complete around you, I said in a low-pitched voice barely above a whisper and a faster heartbeat than ever.

And nothing makes me so happier than when I see you around me, I can lose everything to win you Aarav, she responded.

What if you lose me? I threw a bomb at her.

This can never happen, you are all mine, she said and hugged me tightly.

I will lose myself if I lose you, Swati, I caressed her cheeks.

She slapped me.

She clutched my neck and kissed me. My heart beat started racing, I kissed Swati, I smooched her. She ripped off my shirt and I stripped off her top. I kissed her neck, bit her ears, kissed her eyes, her nose. She quickly started kissing my chest, my neck, and my cheeks. I grabbed her and kissed her again. You know Swati, I am a vampire, I whispered in her ear and began biting her neck. Does not matter, I still love you, she looked into my eyes.

I lifted her into my arms, looking into her eyes, and laid her down on the bed.

I laid on top of her. She was scared, so I calmed her by running my fingers across her face. I whispered, "You are mine, baby."

After exposing herself to me, she kissed my forehead. I could feel her breath. Her legs wrapped around me as I pressed myself closer, our bodies perfectly in sync. I kissed her passionately and deeply until we both got absorbed in each other.

It was just after a few more minutes, the lights of the room went off, and the room became darker, it was again lit up by the spark between both of us. I got physical with Swati ….

The next morning at 6 AM.

Good morning, baby, Swati chirped in my ears. "Good morning love, I responded. She was in my arms, and I was hugging her. This was one of the best days in my life. I could still not imagine she was actually with me, so close to me." Are you not interested in exploring Manali, she asked." I am only genuinely interested in you, but since we are here for 4 days we should explore Manali; otherwise your best friend would curse us, I answered. I kissed her forehead before we woke up and got ready to wander around Manali. We did not sight-see anything in Manali in the previous day. We called in Ridhi, and we dressed up quickly to move out of the hotel at around 9 AM.

The very first thing we got up to was to visit the very famous Hadimba temple. We started off our exploration with prayers. Later on, we headed to the Club house in

Manali. There we were engaged in thrilling activities like boating and go karting, which were very enjoyable.

The next day, we set out to Solang valley, which was idyllic and beautiful. There we had plenty of nerve-wracking experiences that were soul-stirring like paragliding, z orbing, yak riding and more. We enjoyed it a lot, especially Swati. There were countless fun moments altogether.

The next day was the best part of our trip. The much awaited visit to rohtang pass was finally done on the third day of our trip. It was one of the most well-known places to visit in Manali, and we had some of the most wonderful memories to hold on to from there. Swati and I, along with Ridhi, snapped numerous pictures and were enthralled by the whole experience. The best romantic pictures of Swati and I kissing and hugging each other with a dreamy view in the background were clicked by Ridhi, and I instantaneously saved and kept a backup of those romantic pictures in my phone.

25

December 2019

"Hey Swati, are you looking forward to your relative's wedding? I spoke to her on a phone call. I am not yet 100% sure, Aarav, she told me.

A couple of more months went by, and we started getting emotionally attached to each other. I was unable to spend even a single hour without chatting to her. I would impatiently wait for her text messages on what's app, even when it was my office hours. That WhatsApp chirping notification sound was my daily source of euphoria.

We used to exchange plenty of text messages between us all throughout the day. I never missed the chance to catch up and meet her during the evening. I had recently bought a brand-new sports bike of black colour, which was my favourite colour, and I was so excited to make Swati sit on its back seat. I believed that my sports bike would only give a decent mileage when she would sit on it and I would ride. However, I was a bit worried about my father who calls sports bike as nude bike and what if I introduced my new bike to him. Oh, God! I restricted my imagination there itself.

It was the month of December and, as we all know, December is the month of marriage. Someone in Swati's relation was getting married. I did not have an idea who was getting married, since she called it someone. Later she said, it's her cousin who is getting married. All the members of her family, including her parents and Swati herself, had to go to Lucknow for the marriage ceremony. But she had some other plans, she saw this as an opportunity to spend some time with me. She was intelligent. Just a day before they were to leave, she planned and declared herself sick, she told her parents that she is having low fever, and she could not attend the marriage ceremony. Her parents hesitated to leave her alone, but she countered by saying that "it's not ideal to keep the café closed for a week. There is nothing that will happen if I won't attend the ceremony, and moreover, I don't have good relation with my cousins. Instead of staying there and feeling isolated, I can simply remain here and manage the café. She was defending herself like a well-trained lawyer. Her parents tried to convince her, but Swati never loses an argument and she won. It seemed like she liked my company more than her company. I believed her cousins were jealous of her natural beauty.

It was a one-week wedding trip for her parents and brother, and she decided to keep the Agarwal café closed for the first few days to spend time with me. It was close to 7 PM the next day and I picked up Swati from 1 km away distance from her home on my brand-new sports bike. It was ice-cold, and we were wearing our winter jackets, and putting on helmets made us feel secured both from cold and from people. No one would come to recognize us in that shivering cold of Delhi and who would dare to, nobody in this kalyug is that bothered about anyone.

Swati fitted the helmet and got into the back seat of my bike, she gripped my waist, and I set the Bike to gear no 2, and I throttled the accelerator. I was reminiscing about how my dad bike back home denies running faster. But my sports bike after getting Swati on the back seat was like 'chal bhaag Milkha'.

I switched to gear no 3 and sped up the bike, it jerked and Swati too …

I gradually increased the speed of my bike, and Swati held my waist tighter and rested her head on my back.

I deliberately applied the brakes at frequent intervals even when there were no breakers or traffic just because I wanted Swati to jerk me from behind, I succeeded in doing it several times, but she did not utter a single word. I thought that Swati was truly enjoying this, and I continued to do it a few more times with intent, I really did not know this time it would frustrate her to a great extent.

Stop the bike, she raised her voice at me.

Why? What happened? I immediately applied the brakes. I was confused.

If you press the brake for one more time, I would get off and leave here itself, it was a rare dhamki from her.

But there was a breaker Swati, I did not do it on purpose. I tried my best to explain to her.

Even if there is a breaker now, you won't apply the brakes. If you do, I will ride the bike instead of you.

Her words terrorized me, I have seen her applying brakes with her legs on her scooty and she would ride the bike. I closed my eyes and thanked GOD that she had given me a second chance.

But Swati how can I ride the bike without use of brake, I asked her again as it was one of the most challenging tasks to ride a bike without using the brakes.

Alright, fine, I am leaving then, she continued with her dhamki.

Trying to argue with her was similar to arguing with a lawyer. I rest my case, My lord, I responded to her.

I continued my riding and I utilized all my bike riding skills to take as less break as possible so that she does not feel cranky.

I have a news, Aarav? Her voice was barely above a whisper.

What? Good news or bad News? I asked.

Breaking News, she responded.

Your best friend Rohan Gupta and my best friend Ridhi Ahuja are dating each other.

What? What are you saying? How is this possible? I right away applied the brakes and I asked her, concerned.

Yes Aarav, I got to know this from one of my mutual friends, she said. Actually, Ridhi and Rohan were seen together in a restaurant, and I was informed, I know that they are dating, she added.

When did this happen? I asked her in disbelief.

Probably after our Manali trip, she informed me.

I cannot believe this, Rohan is such a big tharki, He eyed on you and then Ridhi, I laughed.

But why did he not speak to me about this, I stay with him in the same flat, what would I have done if I had known this, I really don't know the reason he hid this from me, I continued.

He is your best friend, how would I know why he did not share this with you, she said. Even mine best friend did not share it with me, she added.

You know Swati, Rohan was the one who told me on the first day itself that you were truly interested in me, and you stared at me all the time when I visited your café, I can't believe why he did not share me his dating news, I am shocked.

Oye Tripathi, Who said I was staring at you from day 1, and I was interested in you? Oh, god, she this guy now? She said while playing with her voice.

I straight away got down from my bike and stood in front of Swati and asked, so you don't like me? Were you not interested in me? I asked her several questions back to back.

I like you na, but when did I stare at you when you first came to our café, she raised her eyebrows and questioned in a soft voice.

Rohan and Kreepesh confirmed that you were also staring at me, I answered.

It was because you were continuously looking at me, and I was looking at you back to find out whether you were looking at me or not, and why were you looking at me? She tried her level best to deceive me with her words.

Will you ever allow me to win any argument with you, Swati? If you were a lawyer, then trust me, no other lawyer in this entire world has the audacity to defeat you in an argument.

But I am defeated Aarav, she began to show off her flirting skills to calm me down.

How and when?? I asked.

I am defeated in your love and care for me, you have won me Aarav, she said in a very flirtatious tone.

These words from her sounded like Katha to me, which was sung from her melodious voice.

If I had some salt and mustard seeds, I would have cast off the evil eye there itself.

Okay, fine, It's already getting late now. Before I leave you back home, I have some surprise for you, I said.

And what's that? She was speechless.

Please get down from the bike and I would tell you? I responded.

She got down from the bike very excitedly as if I had surprised something for her in real.

As soon as she got down, I took off her helmet and dropped it on the back seat. I removed mine too. I kissed her soft silky satin-like lips and then handed her helmet back again. I urged her to take her seat.

When she saw this behaviour of mine, she looked at me with a very peculiar sort of expression on her face.

You know Tripathi, you are a bigger tharki than Rohan.

This is a good night kiss, don't you know that, are you still a kid Swati.

She slapped me and it was extremely hard this time ... I decided to drop her at her house because it was almost 10 PM.

I dropped her back home few kms before her house and made my way back to my flat to abuse Rohan.

26

November 2020

After a year...

"Hey guys, can we hang out today in the evening, it's been so long since we have enjoyed hanging out together apart from our office work, I invited both Rohan and Kreepesh to join me at an evening party.

It was one more year, and I was staying close to Agarwal café in Raipur Khadar, sector 126 but all alone in a 1 BHK flat since Rohan was dating Ridhi, and he preferred to stay in a flat that was close to Ridhi's home in sector 44, Noida so that he can meet her everyday. Rohan's current flat was 5 km away from mine and Kreepesh, as usual, was still lodging in a shared flat in a close by location in sector 126. We all three friends embarked our corporate journey together, but we were splintered now. Divided by flats and also in our projects. Rohan, I and Kreepesh were tasked with working on different projects in our company as we had different roles as engineers, and we barely used to get time to stay in touch with each other during office hours or after the work hours. Rohan had left more than 6 months ago to his new flat and had started staying away from me, we hardly had any meaningful conversations after then. I planned to have a meet up and spend some time with both of them.

At the very same time, I did not realize how more than a year passed dating Swati. Our relationship had blossomed over time. I could not even imagine my life without her, and I firmly believed that she would also not. We were able to spend lots of precious time together in this past year and created numerous memories. We barely stayed without chatting online for even an hour. Our deep affection and love for each other grew by each passing day. We used to romance even in text messages and blow kisses all day through emojis. Swati had got too sensitive about me in this recent times and that was reflected in her behaviour. She had become more caring for me. She was in true love with me, and it was my responsibility to keep her happier.

The very next day, Rohan, I and Kreepesh had some incredibly fun moments together as we clubbed together at a rooftop bar and talked about our feelings with each other. We cracked jokes, made fun of each other, and had our most-favoured wine and whiskey. After being together for almost three hours that day and recollecting all our memories, we made our way back to our respective flats.

After a month ...

It was in the month of December, and as we know, December is the wedding season. One of the things I was scared of during those days was marriage, as attending the wedding of someone else would take me to the wedding location where I would marry Swati. However, the wedding location was not confirmed as I had no idea what our future was going to be. I was petrified of losing Swati, the thought of leaving her by any means terrified me as I was so much in love with her. I was invited by my relatives whose daughter was about to get married. I had not visited my home in the past 6 months and hence I was more invested in going back to my home other than attending the marriage ceremony. I informed Swati about myself setting off to Patna for a relatives' marriage, and she retaliated by stating that she made a serious plan to skip her cousin's wedding only to be there with me last year, but I am going to my home to attend the wedding function. However, later I realized that she was teasing me and joking as she said that I should go home and meet my family members first. At certain times, it was very challenging to understand Swati.

I left for my home in a few days…

Patna
As soon as I made it to my home, my parents, and my family were already having arrangements for the marriage function. They were busy in picking out the dress, and gold gifts that they would present to the bride and groom. My mother was frequently attending calls of her sisters and other relatives, and she was clearly very excited about the function. I gave myself a good sleep before I could get ready and leave for the marriage function that was to be held in the evening in a 5-star hotel that was 5 km away from our house in Patna. I, together with my parents, left for the function.

The scheduled function started at around 7 PM with traditional varmala and all that. Frankly, I was not at all active in the function, I was missing Swati badly. I was cocooned in her thoughts, and I was imagining my own varmala with my very own beautiful actress, Mrs Swati. I was literally smiling, and I was wholeheartedly lost in her before my mother came and interrupted me …

Arrange marriage is so amazing Aarav, look how every single person is so happy, she blew up my good mood within a second.

And how did you figure out that everyone is happy here mom, *jo dikhta hai wo hota nahi*, I responded as I turned my eyes towards her.

Look at all the family members how happy they are, look at the bride and groom too, this is how a marriage should be, where everyone's happiness is valued after and not that love marriage where they are no function and none of the family members are happy.

And what about the couples' happiness, are they happy with each other? I asked.

Of course, they are, can't you just look at them, they have their family support too, she added while expressing her delight.

Family support is secondary, the first thing is that the couple should support themselves in tough and good times both and this is only possible when they are in love and genuinely care for each other, I told her.

After arranged marriage, you are bound to fall in love with your partner, even if you're not, you will fall in love when you have your kids, she responded.

In our olden days, we were not permitted to even talk to the groom before marriage, but see how those marriages are successful and not like the modern love marriages where the divorce rate is so high, she added.

So you still think that time has not progressed, we still say "I love you" to someone with a love letter packed in an envelope and pass it to them to get their handwritten response, my mother got displeased with my words.

What are you trying to say, Aarav? She asked confusedly.

If people after arrange marriage are bound to fall in love with their partners because they spend so much time together, then people of this modern age who use digital communication, social media and are connected to calls with their love partners every single day are also bound to fall in love and their emotions would be much, much higher, if this happens, then what would a parent go for, everyone's happiness or their child's happiness or wait for their grown adult child to have a kid, and fall in love with their arranged partner, what do you have to say about this, I responded to her, the conversation was getting extremely heated.

Aarav, what are you trying to say. Are you against arrange marriage, are you getting married to someone you love, she raised her voice.

Did I Say that I am getting married to someone else? I said in a bitter tone.

My only question is how can you get married to someone even without knowing each other, what if the marriage goes horribly wrong and there are compatibility issues, there is no love and care between them, I quizzed her.

Did the marriages gone wrong in our times, where there was no communication with bride and groom what's so ever, don't they have a beautiful family, she repeated this sentence.

The marriages did not go wrong in those times because the girl was taught that' he is your husband" and no matter whatever you go through in your life, you should stay with him as our home is not yours any more and even after having to struggle so much in their married life, people used to hold on to their marriage for the sake of society. The same thing applies for husbands too, where they carry on their relationship even if they are not happy or are in an abusive relationship. Now please don't tell me that every people who married in those times had a happy married life, don't you think it's a compromise, I responded.

We can have kids even without genuinely loving each other, I added.

Are you trying to defend love marriage, don't you know that your father will kick you out of the house if you go against him, she replied in a stern tone.

Thanks for reminding me that, I will take care, I responded, and I was incensed.

I walked away without mouthing a single word and having any further conversation with any other person what's so ever.

Swati was everything to me. I did not have any idea who was right between me and my mom, or either arrange marriage or love marriage, all that I did know was that Swati was the right girl for me. She loved me and she cared for me. She connected with me so well, she guides me to be a good human-being and what else does a man need. I felt I was very fortunate to have her in my life. I did not want this arrange marriage and love marriage drama at all. I will marry Swati and will convince everyone for it, I promised to myself. I was sure if my family members would ever meet Swati, they would never deny her as she was the sweetest girl one can ever meet. The only thing that was bothering me was my father, he was a stern man. I can take care of everyone in my family and until date, I have got almost everything in my life which I desired. But I also desired Swati. I knew it's almost impossible to convince my father for a love marriage. He loved me, but he has always lived with that pride and was a total society man. I can understand that from his point, but I was already in love with Swati. He would not forgive me if I entered into a love marriage. I found myself stressed and that was the reason I made the decision to get out of my home after a couple of days only rather than my scheduled week stay. I loved my parents and I loved Swati too. I only prayed to god to keep all the people happy, but I can't live without Swati, I will die if I see her with someone else, I thought this so many times. Even if my heart beat keeps going, my soul will leave my body if it does not find her around me.

27

"Hi Swati I am not feeling well, can you please meet me a bit early at the café today, I requested her on a phone call. She responded" Why what happened, is everything good ". Everything is all right, just wanting to meet you, I said and hung up the phone call.

Once I got back to Delhi from Patna, I was very stressed about my relationship. I had plenty of questions lingering in my mind, such as whether I would be allowed to go for love marriage or not, or will I be able to marry Swati in an arrange marriage setup. There was lot of overthinking activity going on in my mind. I had become miffed thinking about all these problems. It was also not any good at my office, as I was unable to focus on my work because of too much thinking. I was afraid. All this overexertion stung me a lot, and I was not in a pleasant mood. I can't dream of my life without Swati even in my worst of dreams. I loved her truly and prayed to get her for my whole life, and I would climb mountains for that, but how? Should I kill my family's happiness, or should I kill my relationship, or at the end, should I kill myself? I didn't understand why these questions were growing in my mind ...

It was close to 6 PM the same day, and I had skipped my office for the past 2 days because of my terribly depressed mood. I had called Swati to the café earlier that day. I headed to the Agarwal café from my flat and upon reaching I could see Swati was already there way before her usual time. I strolled straight to her.

Swati, get me an adrak chai, I am having a headache, I told her.

She called Rahul and asked him to deliver me the tea as soon as possible. She responded, "Is everything alright, Aarav."

Everything is fine, Swati.

You look upset, she said.

It's office work pressure nothing else, I lied to her.

But you have been absent from your office for the past 2 days, right, she asked.

What are you doing alone at your flat, she added, as she was confused and surprised.

But I am still working on my office projects from my flat even though I am absent from the office, it's stressful.

Are you hiding something from me, she raised her eyebrows.

Why would I hide anything from you, Swati.

Is there any family problem, Aarav?

Not at all Swati, I was there at my home for only a few days, what would go wrong, everything is fine, I lied to her.

But you were supposed to stay for a week at your home and I forgot to ask you why did you come back so suddenly within a couple of days, you can be honest with me Aarav, I am not a stranger to you, she told me.

It seems you are hiding something, you are completely out of your natural behaviour, she added after getting no response from me.

Swati, you are unnecessarily trying to dig out a thriller story from my case here, everything is fine, could you please get me my chai, I requested her while diverting her from the topic.

Meanwhile, Rahul brought in the tea and I began sipping slowly. I was so depressed that I was not even looking at Swati, and she had already noticed that.

You know Tripathi ji, you are not happy. She looked at me.

And how can you confirm that? I responded.

I will not confirm that, I already know that, hence Mr Tripathi, I have some surprise in store for you? She said in an excitement-filled tone. She was doing her best to uplift my mood.

What's the plan, I replied in a very hushed tone.

I am going to take you on a ride? She seemed very excited about it.

What! You are taking me on a ride, or I should take you on a ride? I did not understand this point, Swati? I was confused.

I am taking you on a ride on my scooty, better you go and get your ear check up done, She told me.

I laughed so loud, and My teeth glistened, have you taken' ganza' Swati? Are you alright? I could not stop myself from breaking out in laughter.

Not everyone, like you engineers, are interested in 'ganza' alright. I am perfectly fine, I am taking you on a ride and that's final, I can't see you unhappy, she responded.

I am not unhappy, I told her after remembering her riding skills.

What if you apply brakes with your legs, and it makes a screeching sound, will it be a good scooty ride? I added again.

Can you please shut up now, I have passed the driving test three times.

So you failed the first two attempts, I was seriously worried.

Shut up, I have 3 years of experience in riding scooty, don't you know that, I am comfortable going on a long ride and I have done that in the past too with Ridhi, she lied professionally about her driving skills.

Oh, so you are planning for a long ride, I was curious.

Yes, We are riding on our scooty to Varanasi via road, Mr. Tripathi. It would be such a great fun, she yelled mellowly.

Oh Swati, have you gone out of your mind, Varanasi is 800 KMS away from Delhi and you want to take me via road that too on your scooty where you would be applying brakes with your legs? I can wait for Yamraj, please allow me to get back to my flat, you are not well, I pleaded with her.

Just shut up your mouth, don't speak a word, I will show you my riding talent, don't you worry, she raised her voice.

I should be alive to see that, I taunted her.

As soon as I said this, she placed her hand to my mouth. Get ready Tomorrow at around 6 AM. I will be there right under your flat.

Did you get that? She said again.

But Swati? I have missed my office for these two days, another leave, I replied.

No if and but, just be there. If you don't go with me, then never talk to me, she pulled out her sword.

After having a long talk with her, I made my way back to my flat. I had come to her café in a very unpleasant mood, but she has somehow managed to enlighten my mood. However, her "Mountain Dew darr k aage jeet hai" plan scared me a lot. She planned for a long drive to Varanasi, that too in the winters. Varanasi was 800 km away from Delhi. The worst part was that she had chosen her small scooty for this ride, which would hurt my ass a lot while sitting at the back seat. I could have driven her to Varanasi on my bike, but I cannot argue with her, as I will surely not win. I thought Swati had gone crazy. I was a bit sad. I was unhappy, and I was overthinking, and she planned this only to keep me happy. I already knew she never loses a game and an argument, and she might have made another plan and lied to convince her parents for this dangerous trip. It will be a pain in my ass to sit on the back seat of her small scooty. But I would bear that pain any day for my love Swati. I was afraid, at the same time very excited.

28

"You fool, I am calling you for so long, why don't you pick up the phone? I am going to arrive in 20 minutes, get ready quickly, she shouted at me on the phone call.

It was close to 5 AM and I could not even open my eyes. There were 10 missed calls from Swati. As soon as I woke up and noticed that, I was in a state of terror. She informed me that she would be arriving in the next 20 minutes. I hurriedly went to shower which was one of the toughest tasks I had ever done and having a shower in the morning was like attaining a vibe of *Narak* on earth. I rushed to dress up. It was a three-day trip as stated by her, so we were going to stay in Varanasi for a single day and the rest of two days would be devoted to riding. I began packing my bags and was waiting for her to arrive. The only thing that bugged me was the distance that was 800 KMS away from Delhi, and we were riding by road. However, I could do nothing but to accompany her to the trip because I loved her.

It was shortly before 6 AM, I received a call from Swati." Come down quickly", she commanded on the call. I moved towards the open window of my room and glanced down to see her. She was there waiting for me with her scooty wearing a helmet. She was waving at me and I gestured to her with my hands that I was coming down. I also signalled the killing sign with my hands, to which she could not stop herself from breaking out in raucous laughter.

I speedily stepped down from my flat, and she handed me my helmet. Before she could start riding, I wanted to ask her something.

You are a liar, I told her.

Oh God, why are you saying this to me? She responded.

You said you will be here in 20 minutes, and you took 1 hour to arrive, is it not a lie?

I said that because I wanted you to get ready as soon as possible, I know how tough is it for you to wake up early in the morning, I did that so that we won't get late, she told me.

But you should have told the truth to me, why to lie for such small reasons, I asked her again.

Will you sit or not? Don't argue with me, wear the helmet and sit on the back seat, she threatened me again.

I buckled the helmet and settled into the rigid back seat of her scooty. It took me some time to adjust my ass.

Can you please show me Swati how would you apply brakes? I made fun of her.

She applied the brake right away, and I jerked at her. I suspected that she was seeking revenge from me.

Why are you doing this? This is how you will apply the brakes on a long ride? I am very nervous now about your riding skills.

She flicked the accelerator, it was early in the morning, and it was chilly, and we were on the highway. She rocketed the scooty to around 75 km/ hour. The highest speed that her scooty had was 80 km/hour, which was only 5 km/hr less than what she was riding. I got panicked. I vividly remembered an instance when she imbalanced the scooty on a very busy road and an old man who was walking in front of her just begged for mercy with his folded hands. That kind of dangerous rider she was.

You can't be a pro rider unless you know how to ride fast, she claimed herself as a pro rider.

We are not racing here, please remember that, please ride slow, I was pleading with her while paying attention to the speed metre.

Are you afraid? She asked.

No, I am not afraid, I responded.

If you are not afraid, then I won't be riding slow.

Afraid? I am terrorized Swati, I will pee in my pants, please slow down the speed and apply brakes and forgive me, I pleaded her with folded hands.

She showed some sympathy and throttled down the speed, and I took a big sigh of relief.

This was an 800 KM long ride; we frequently headed over to nearby dhabas and tea shops, as we could not sustain ourselves without tea. I was scared when we started the journey, but it turned out to be super fun. It was going to take us around 13 hours to reach Varanasi from Delhi. We took off at around 6 AM, that meant we would reach it at around 7 PM. However, we had many chai samosa breaks in between.

It was closer to 3 PM, and it had started drizzling heavily, it got gloomy, and there was a lot of pain in my ass while seated at the back seat of a small scooty, I even complained about this to her, but she rejected me plea. I had never sat that long even in my college or office, I did not have that kind of patience, but I had to keep going. I was missing my sports bike. The journey was getting boring and hence she decided to make fun of mine, and she came up with a "truth or dare" game. The game rule was that it would be played while on the journey to Varanasi and also while returning back from Varanasi so that the trip does not get boring and that we would confess something that's still unknown to us.

Truth or dare? She asked.

I would rather not say anything, of truth. I was already thinking too much in my mind about my relationship with her, and I also can't lie to her, I said dare.

As soon she heard dare, she got fired up, she instantly applied the brakes and ordered me to get down from her scooty. I got scared. There was none on the road.

Please get down and come to the front? She said as she cocked her head towards me.

Why Swati, what happened. Why should I get down?

Just get down and come forward, it's my order.

Okay, I responded.

I got down from the scooty and stood in front of her, it was drizzling very heavily, and I had still not taken off my helmets to protect myself from the heavy rain.

Common Aarav show me your dancing skills now, just dance. She pulled out her phone and hurried to play "Dance basanti" song on YouTube.

What's this behaviour Swati, what are you doing and why this song Dance Basanti, I am a Nar not a Maada, please play a song that is related to me.

Will you dance or should I leave you and go, she threatened me again.

Luckily, there were none of the people watching us because of the heavy rainfall. The roads were empty of people.

I visualized the dancing steps of Shraddha Kapoor in Dance Basanti and I tried my best to imitate it. I was not at a good dancer and I knew that. She just made me feel so uncomfortable.

Every single time I tried to replicate steps, Swati laughed like a judge of a struggling comedy show. Her eyes got watery because of excessive laughing. I just took the back seat and chose to keep my mouth shut.

It was close to 8 PM, and we made it to Varanasi, it was freezing cold. We made the decision not to visit any ghats that day and to have some rest. She had already booked a hotel, and we checked inside the hotel at 8:30 PM. I was still wondering how did she manage to check in late evening. She had executed her plans very well. Our next plan was to roam ghats and visit temples the next day and then leave back to Delhi the very next day. Although I was with Swati, but my mind was still somewhere back home, I was still mulling over the conversation with my mother. It was painful inside, and I could not explain how was the pain, I had sensations of severe pain vibrating throughout my body while I was thinking about all these things. I can bear any pain, but I cannot bear the pain of losing Swati. She was my soul. Whole night I hugged her and slept: She understood that something was not okay, she asked me so many times if there was any reason, but I was a superb actor.

It was close to 10 AM the next day and I woke up. I had a mild fever the entire night. I ordered my tea, and meanwhile I saw Swati entering the room with some fruits and medicine. I was hesitant to eat those, but she forced me to eat. After having a biscuit and chai, I ate some mixed fruits that she brought, and then she gave me a paracetamol, which I swallowed with water. The only thing I was able to recall that day, was that for the entire night she inspected my head while rubbing her palms to my forehead to see if I had a high fever or not. She loved me a lot and her care for me was increasing day by day.

I was just staring at her, and my love for her was increasing each day. I was sick, so we could not go anywhere in the noon time, and hence we decided to travel to the ghats and have a boat ride during the evening when the view would be mesmerizing.

It was just after 7 PM, and we passed by a few ghats of Varanasi and Varanasi truly was a place of great serenity, and then it was time to take the most famous boat ride. We booked the boat for 2 people and trust me, it was one of the best rides I can ever have. Varanasi was such a beautiful place, and we took some incredible selfies together.

How's the place, Aarav, she inquired as she turned her eyes towards me while sitting on the boat.

It's truly wonderful Swati, very peaceful, anyone can rest in peace here, I said in a joking tone.

Don't joke, she raised her voice.

Did you like my plan?

Yeah, I liked

Do you have something to share, she toned down her voice this time.

No Swati.

I tried my best to divert her from this topic.

This place is so peaceful na but Swati, travelling 800 KMS by road that too on a scooty, I must have done this journey on my bike, and it would not have been a pain in my ass, I tried to lighten the mood.

It was my plan Aarav, so I wanted to ride and take you to Varanasi and I don't ride a bike or drive a car, hence scooty was the only option for me.

Is there anything that you are hiding from me? She picked up the dangerous topic again.

No Swati why would I even do that?

But you look so worried? What's the matter?

I am stressed about my office work and nothing else, I lied to her.

You will never leave me na, I can't live without you Aarav, I will die if this happens. I was finding it very hard to hold back my emotions.

Swati If I am alive, I will always be with you, consider me dead if I ever leave you alone, I held her hands.

For the first time, I saw Swati in fear, seeing her like this tore my heart into shattered pieces, she was the person who used to always remain positive and joyful. But she was teary that day. I could not gaze at her eyes, I was not that strong enough.

After half an hour.

The conversation was so emotionally charged that it broke both of us. We made our way back to our hotel room, and we were upset. We were leaving the next morning back to Delhi, so we slept at around 10 PM, and we did not have our dinner that day.

It was about 6 AM, and we set off for Delhi. As usual, we had some chai and snacks at nearby dhabas and Swati rode the scooty. After 5 hours of non-stop riding, it was getting boring again. We did not have much of a conversation on the return trip, and we did not know why. Probably, both Swati and I were thinking too much about something on our head that we couldn't explain to each other.

Let's continue the "truth and dare" game, Aarav, Swati spoke to me after a very long silence.

But I don't want to dance, I responded.

Who said you to dance, it was a "dare" previous time and this time the automatic choice is truth.

Okay, I said.

Yes, but there is a condition this time? She added.

And What's that condition.

You are swearing by me that whatever you will say will be true, she responded.

OK. I responded, as I had no other options left. I loved her so much, and I could not lie.

What's your biggest fear regarding me, she asked.

This question came like a bullet to me, piercing my heart and carving a hole there. I hesitated.

I was unable to speak. I shuddered. I was unresponsive. I went into silence.

Why are you silent, taking my swear has no value to you, right? She was in anger.

My deepest fear regarding you is.

What? She asked.

Your Wedding, I spoke in a very low-key voice. I was in a lot of pain.

How can 'my wedding' be your deepest fear' that too regarding me, you should be happy about it, she asked a clarification.

I don't know who will be your partner on your wedding day, I said, and my soul wept.

Swati went numb, she was quiet, she did not utter a word.

So you are not going to marry me, right? She spoke again after a few minutes of complete silence.

Swati I love you, that is the reason I fear losing you, I said.

But why are you so afraid of losing me, what's the reason, she asked.

There is no reason, Swati, I responded.

If you ever again lie to me, I would die in front of you, take this as a curse. Tell me the truth now, I want to listen.

Swati, I hesitated.

What's the truth, she asked.

I am a brahmin, I responded.

So what Aarav, don't I know that, she said.

Love marriages are not allowed in my family if the partner is not brahmin, I spoke in a very low voice.

There was complete silence. I could sense Swati struggling to talk further.

But time has changed Swati, I promise I will convince my parents, I will never go away from you, I said.

What if you do? She asked.

Then I will run and come back to you again, I told her.

Swati let's not worry about this too much, it's modern age and I promise I would convince everyone to marry you or else I would prefer dying. In fact, many of them are doing inter-caste marriages now. It's not a big deal, I tried to calm her emotions down.

She rode scooty for another hour without saying a word, and we both were silent. It was drizzling again and Swati took the bizarre route which was not there in the Google map.

You are taking the wrong route, Swati, I asked her confusedly.

She did not answer.

She rode the scooty on a very secluded road, and she got off from the scooty, I was still sitting at the back seat. She asked me to get down. I was puzzled, I mounted the scooty to its stand, removed mine helmet and stood closer to her.

She took off her helmet and placed it on the seat of the scooty.

She wrapped her arms around my waist and hugged me tightly. She rested her head on my chest.

I love you Aarav, I would rather not live this life without you, you promise me you won't leave me? She was in floods of tears.

I could not stop my tears from sliding down my eyes. I kissed her on the forehead.

I promise you Swati, I will climb mountains to marry you, I can go to any extent to get you in my life, please don't cry, I am always with you. I am yours, and you are only mine.

What if you don't Aarav, she asked.

So you are saying, you won't dance and show your dancing skills on our wedding day, I intended to calm her.

I will, I am a good dancer, you know that, she said with her struggling voice.

Absolutely, I responded.

She blushed but was still crying.

She kissed me and I gently stroked her lips. We both closed our eyes, and we were lost for some time as we hugged each other tightly.

I had bought something for you, Swati, I told her after a few minutes.

What? She expressed interest.

I took out a beautiful *blue colour bracelet* from my pocket which I had bought for her from the city of love, Varanasi and showed it to her.

It's beautiful Aarav, when did you buy it, she was curious.

I bought it to gift it to you, but I will not gift you now, I want you to wear this on your wedding day, I kissed her forehead.

She hugged me with all the love that she had.

I love you Swati, I showed all my love to her, and we continued on our journey back to Delhi. I made her comfortable, and I made sure to make her happy by cracking jokes at the leftover journey. I was successful in making her laugh and assuring her that everything will be alright in the end, and we will get married.

29

Hey what happened? Are you okay, Swati ? I was concerned about her health, I was on the phone call. "Nothing very serious, Aarav, I am suffering from a viral fever", she informed me. "Please take good care of yourself, baby", I suggested. "A Lot of many people are having some sort of

She Was Only Mine

viral fever or flu, I guess", I added. "Yes babe, I have taken the medicine, hopefully it will take a couple of more days for me to get back to the café, she responded." You know I am missing you so badly, I told her while expressing my sadness." I will be getting back soon Aaru, Okay I am leaving now, she said on the call.

Chai piya tune, did you have your tea, she asked.

Nope, I have got a bit late at the office today, I can't sip tea without looking at you in front of my eyes' babe, I only love 'swatiest chai', don't you already know that, I said her being flirty.

Less acting please, Go and have it somewhere, I am leaving now, she whispered and smooched me on the call.

I blew some kisses while sitting in my office and hung up the call.

It was the final week of January, and most people at that time were getting sick with some sort of viral fever or flu. Even some of my colleagues had got sick. I was myself struggling with a cough and cold. I understood that it was the viral flu that was driving people to get sick. Swati was sick too and was absent from her Agarwal café for the past 2 days, and I was missing her immensely. Her elder brother Abhay was managing the café both in the morning and evening. The café turned very dull without Swati. Having nothing else to do in the evening without her being present at the café made me feel very jaded.

It was close to 7:30 PM and I got very late at the office. I was heading back to my flat from my office on my sports bike. At that moment, I glanced at Kreepesh who was waiting outside the HCL campus and the reason behind it was unknown to me. I instantly called in Kreepesh while waving at him to come with me since I had not met him personally for a very long time. I just wanted to know how he was and how he was going in his life. I stopped for a few more minutes before Kreepesh jumped on my bike and I began to accelerate." Chal saath mei chai peete hai", I said to him." Bhot din ho gya yaar saath mei, he spoke with a sense of excitement. I picked him from the HCL campus and rode to sector 126 where we halted at 'chai sutta bar'.

It was close to 8 PM and I and Kreepesh both were having some meaningful conversation at "chai sutta bar" while sipping on our tea and some snacks in hand. It was good to reconnect with Kreepesh after a very long time. However, he was still unhappy with his personal life. He has not got any hikes and was finding it difficult to work on projects because of his bad communication skills. I did not try to delve deeper into his personal life. After sometime, He asked about me and Swati's relationship, which I said it's going very well, and I am so happy with her. However, He looked very upset. I tried my best to uplift his mood, but he was all the time just harping on his dire financial condition and personal life, which made me feel out of place; hence I decided to go back to my flat. After having some talk with him for half an hour, it was 8:40 PM, and we were about to head back to our respective flats.

I made payment for the bill, and I was all set to leave. Kreepesh and I hugged and were about to head back to our respective flats. However, we both stayed in sector 126, but we hardly met. It felt good talking to him and spending some time together. I decided to head back to my flat as I was already frazzled after long hours at the office.

As soon as I walked a few steps forward and was about to get to my bike, I came across Ridhi passing by me, and she was shivering with cold. I didn't have any idea what had happened to her. I and Kreepesh hurriedly moved closer to her.

Hey Ridhi, what happened, why are you shivering so much, I asked her worriedly.

Actually, I have picked up fever, I was invited by one of my close college friend on her birthday party, but I got sick, she said with her voice shaking.

So why did you turn up to her birthday party, Ridhi, if you were not feeling well, I asked confused.

I told my friend that I am not feeling well, but still, she said I have to be there at her party; otherwise we will have no friendship any more. For the sake of our friendship, I went to the party, but I am not at all feeling well, I am experiencing a high fever, she explained to me the reason.

Even Swati is sick, I shared with her.

Where are you going now? I asked her.

I have booked a cab, but the driver is taking so long to arrive, she told me.

Does Rohan know all about this, I asked her.

He is not here, he has gone to his home and will return in few days, I have spoken to Rohan on the phone call, she told me.

Don't worry Ridhi, I will drop you to your home, I added.

That is so sweet of you Aarav, but I will get to my home myself, my cab would be arriving in a matter of minutes, she said.

You are sick Ridhi, and you should not travel on your own right now, let me drop you please, I told her since she seemed very unwell.

No Aarav, I will go, she replied.

You helped us to our Manali trip, and I am genuinely grateful to you for that, I will never forget your kindness, I told.

Please let me help you this time, I am like your friend, I said.

Meanwhile, Kreepesh looked at me very enigmatically, and I did not understand why.

I asked Kreepesh to head back to his flat.

I picked up Ridhi on my bike and flicked the accelerator. I asked her to cancel the cab. I moved to not more than 100 metres and headed to a nearby medical store, I bought a few medicines for her rising fever from the store.

As I made a turn towards my back after paying the medical store, to my amazement, I noticed that Kreepesh was still following me. He was attentively looking at me from a long distance. As soon as I noticed him, he cocked his head to the opposite direction and started sprinting forward. I was greatly stupefied by his behaviour.

I picked up Ridhi again after buying her medicines and I decided to drop her at her house in Sector 44.

It's very sweet of you Aarav, thank you so much for this, she thanked me after I dropped her to her home.

No mention please, I responded.

Swati is very blessed to have you in her life, I am very happy for her. She added.

Indeed, she is, I got the opportunity to show off my caring nature.

After I dropped her at her house, I headed back to my flat at a breakneck speed because I was getting late.

I began to feel very fatigued as soon as I arrived at my flat. But one specific thing that was troubling me was Kreepesh unusual behaviour. He looked so mysteriously at me when I was having a conversation to Ridhi at the medical store, and I believed that he also followed me to the medical store. I could not figure out what might be the reason. After wasting so much time thinking about him, I got so hungry that I decided to eat my dinner and then go to bed because I had my office the other day. I called Swati and asked her about her fever and health, and exchanged a few kisses with her on the phone call before I fell asleep.

30

After Few Days.....

M**dh*rc*od, how dare you, Rohan came charging at me and grabbed my collar as soon as I stepped inside my office.

Hey, Hold back bro, what happened?, I loosened his hand from my collar, I was completely dumbfounded and shocked at his aggressive behaviour towards me.

How dare you take Ridhi with you on your bike? He was yelling at me and everyone huddled around us.

Bro, I dropped her at her house because she was feeling ill, instead of thanking me, you are abusing me, I told him.

Don't cover up, you M**dh*rc*od, what were you doing at the medical shop with her, he screamed at me again.

I bought her a few medicines for fever, that's it, I informed him. I was still reticent and wanted to sort out the matter.

Condom kharid raha tha M**dh*rc*od medical store pe, were you buying condoms at the medical store, he gripped my neck.

Stop it M**dh*rc*od, what nonsense are you ranting about, have you lost your mind, I got pissed and I pushed him.

Kreepesh has told me everything, don't lie, Rohan shrieked.

B*h*nc*od Kreepesh told you that I was looking for condoms, M**dh*rc*od, I lashed out at him.

Why were you keen on getting Ridhi on your bike when she was refusing to go with you, he said.

Because she was unwell, and I did not want her to go alone, and nothing else, I responded, but I was suffused with anger.

Who the hell are you to decide whether she should go alone or not, are you her boyfriend?, he clutched my neck again.

I helped her just as a friend, that's all, what's wrong in that, I said.

Because she helped you in Manali trip, that's why, right, Mr. Aarav Tripathi? He responded.

So Kreepesh had told you everything, I added.

You don't even miss a chance to flirt your friend's girlfriend, right? He sought answers.

I was not flirting with her, you better go and ask Ridhi herself, I replied.

Why should I believe you, he asked.

Bro, I have someone like Swati in my life, why would I be even interested In Ridhi, I told him.

Ohh so you think Swati is the best girl in the world, not everyone is like her who sits in her café only to stare at all the guys around, he laughed, and my anger turned violent.

Don't cross your limits, Rohan, I am reminding you, I said ferociously.

Why did you take Ridhi to Manali alone, he asked.

She accompanied us to Manali and nothing else, I informed him.

I asked Why did you take her ?, should I take Swati with me to a trip with Ridhi? Will you allow her with me? Will you not feel bad? He asked again.

You did not disclose to me that you were dating Ridhi that time; otherwise I would have not taken her, I responded.

There is a reason that I did not tell you about my relationship with Ridhi because I know you very well, he said.

What would I have done if I have been aware that Ridhi is your girlfriend, you were living with me for so long in the same flat, and you still have so much dirt about me in your head, I replied.

Fine that you did not know about me and Ridhi during the Manali trip, leave that aside, but today you know that she is my girlfriend still you dropped her alone on your bike to her house putting Kreepesh out of sight so that no one can find out your true intentions. He told. Should I take Swati on my bike and roam around? Will you like that? Just tell me, he was indignant.

Don't bring In Swati to this matter, I am rebuking you again. My blood was bubbling with anger.

Why did you ask Kreepesh to go away to his flat so that you can take Ridhi anywhere you want and flirt with her, why did you get scared when you noticed that Kreepesh was looking at you at the medical store, what were you buying at the medical store? Were you looking to sleep with her? He asked.

Just shut up M**dh*rc*od, don't narrate a false story, you are getting me mad now, I said.

You could have arranged her a cab and dropped to her house along with Kreepesh if you were so concerned about her health, but no, you decided to send Kreepesh away, and you went to the medical store, and you dropped her alone to her house that too on your bike. You took her to Manali for no reason, and you still think I should trust your false story, you are not a saint and I know that very well, he added.

Calm down Rohan, there is no such thing as you are speculating, I tried to calm him down.

M**dh*rc*od you took her on your bike for no reason, fuck your girlfriend, not mine, he screamed at me and this was more than enough to get my blood boil over.

M**dh*rc*od don't talk nonsense about Swati. I will kill you here itself, jaan se maar dunga b*he*c*od, I clutched his neck and smacked him on his face.

I grabbed him and shoved him towards the wall holding his neck and punched him a dozen times, he tried to defend himself with his legs and he kicked my abdomen with his long pointed leather shoes, I writhed in pain, but I couldn't hear any hurtful words about Swati. I stood up and smacked him hard on his nose. He started to bleed from his nose. I punched him on his face, I had no sympathy left for him. Meanwhile, everyone around us watching the fight came to rescue, and they pulled both of us from behind. If I had got few more minutes, I would have killed that Madarchod in the office itself.

My blood was boiling at the biggest M**dh*rc*od Kreepesh, he conspired to make up a false story to foment problems in my life, and he was absent from the office. I would have crushed that Behenchod to death. He was the prime reason for this pointless fight. That jealous Madarchod tried to ruin my life.

M**dh*rc*od, don't you say anything about Swati, M**dh*rc*od stay in your limits, I shouted at him again from a distance while someone grabbed me from the back to avoid the fight.

I pushed away the people who were encircling him and rushed to beat him again. It was getting heated and soon the office Manager arrived.

Baap ka ghar hai ye, the office manager abused.

I am suspending you both for the next 7 days, resolve your fight and then come back here if you want to continue here or else you will get kicked out. Keep, that, in mind. He raised his voice. I turned to look at Rohan for one more time, only because he got saved that day; otherwise I would have taken him to the deathbed.

Now leave …the office manager shouted again.

I stepped out of my office full of rage and got to my bike and I left straight away with a skyrocket speed back to my flat." Fuck this job, I don't care about my job, I will not allow anyone to talk ill about Swati, I love her, I mumbled to myself while riding my bike. For an instance, I thought of driving to Kreepesh flat and fuck that M**dh*rc*od, but I decided to cool myself down as I was furious. Kreepesh was absent that day since he knew there would be something taking place in the office. M**dh*rc*od Kreepesh, I abused him again while driving my bike."Tujhe jaan se maar dalunga b*he*c*od phir life insurance ka paise milenge dalle, I always got the feeling that this "silent M**dh*rc*od Kreepesh" was jealous of me, and he made sure that he gets me into trouble. I speculated that Kreepesh twisted the entire conversation I had with Ridhi and narrated a false story to Rohan that made him angry. I went to my flat thinking about what had just happened. If Kreepesh had been present at the office, I would most probably have strangulated that M**dh*rc*od to death there itself.

31

After a few days.....
'Everything is finished Aarav', *"sab khatam ho gaya"*, Swati spoke to me on the call with her wobbling voice. "Why what happened Swati", I asked her, and I was scared". Someone has shared our private Manali photos to my brother Abhay with some faux account on Instagram", I don't yet know who's that, she told me while weeping." Who's that guy, Swati? And how did he manage to access our Manali Photos, I questioned her, and I was frantic."

I don't have any idea Aarav, papa and Abhay are both mad at you, they have asked me not to meet you ever again and even not to manage the café any more, I am panicking Aarav "she broke down." Hold on Swati, please don't cry, I will find out who that guy is "I tried my best to calm her down. As soon as I wanted to speak something more, the call was cut off from her side. I tried to call her back, but she did not respond to my call. I was nervous, and I did not know what I should do next. I threw all the close-by things in frustration.

After calming my head that was full of anxiety and worry, I lied down on my bed and wanted to find out what had just happened and why it happened. After a little while, I suddenly realized that it was Ridhi who had snapped a lot of pictures of Swati and me when we were on the Manali trip and I asked her to delete those pictures after sending me, but I believed she did not delete it. Rohan, might be the one who shared those photos with Swati's brother because he was the only one who knew Abhay personally and interacted with him more often. Rohan did this out of revenge because of the terrible fight we had in the office regarding Ridhi. Nobody knew Swati's brother apart from Rohan. I also theorized that Rohan might have forced Ridhi to send those photos to him." M**dh*rc*od, Rohan, I shouted with all the power I had. The more I thought about Swati, I started shaking with fear. I had never seen Swati speaking in such a way. I should have not fought with Rohan, I should have controlled my anger, I should have not abused him, I slapped myself for having a fight with Rohan and getting our relationship in a lot of trouble. I roamed around my room full of emotions and anxiety and then laid down on my bed, only to burst into tears.

I didn't know what I should do next. I was very concerned about Swati, I had no idea what she might be struggling through at her home and how she might be dealing with the situation. She sounded very scared on the phone call. I could not even speak to her for 5 minutes. I felt very poorly, and could not hold back my tears.

I will never ever forgive you M**dh*rc*od Rohan, I screamed with a storm of tears rolling out of my eyes.

I never thought that I was destined to live with two of the biggest M**dh*rc*ods, Rohan and Kreepesh, in the same flat. I always sensed that they were jealous of me, especially Kreepesh, but they destroyed me completely in every way. I could have coped with any hardship, but I cannot handle the agony of losing Swati. I cannot live without her. I wanted to ask Swati that what was going in at her home. That silent motherfucker Kreepesh had exposed his true colours at the worst time. I felt like time stood still and everything around me was frozen. After going through a lot with my emotions, it was 12 AM and I received another call from Swati.

Everything is destroyed, Aarav, She cried out.

What happened, Swati, I asked worriedly.

Abhay and papa are furious at me, she said, crying.

What did he say, I asked her.

He did not utter anything, but he asked me not to talk to you any more, and I will not be allowed to go to the café, she said.

I can't leave without you, I had tears in my eyes.

I suggested to you that I don't want to go to Manali alone, but you were not keen on understanding anything, now look at the situation, she continued breaking down on the call.

I did not expect this to happen Swati, it's Ridhi who might have shared photos to Rohan, and he shared it with your brother, I told her.

But why did he do that, he was your best friend, why would he share those photos to my family, she asked.

Swati, I was hesitant.

Tell me why? What are you hiding? She asked irritably.

I had a serious fight with Rohan at the office because Kreepesh told him something that was false about me, and we had a heated argument, that might be the reason he shared our photos to your family out of revenge, I explained her half-baked story so that I don't hurt her any more.

Oh Aarav, why don't you control your anger wherever you go, do you know what have you done, she raised her voice.

I am sorry, Swati, I said.

What sorry, My father is very strict regarding love marriage, and you don't know that, he has seen all our photos of Manali, and it looked as though he was very angry, but he held back his anger, she added.

Swati, please do something, I am scared, I told her.

He asked me to stay at my home, and my brother is mad at you, she said.

What to do next, Swati, I asked

You leave your flat right away or my brother can sneak into your flat, I was seriously worried.

Who will tell him my flat address, I asker her.

The same guy who shared our Manali photos, she said.

I am worried, Swati.

What was the reason that you fought with Rohan, will you let me know please, a small fight cannot get him to do what he has done, she spoke and she was angry.

Actually, Swati when you were away for two days at the café, I called in Kreepesh to join me. That day I found Ridhi returning from a birthday party and walking on the streets with a high fever and I dropped her at her house on my bike, that's it. Kreepesh twisted words and narrated a false story to Rohan, and we got into a massive fight at the office, and I am suspended for 7 days, I explained everything.

Ohh, so you are suspended too, why don't you tell me everything, she said in a loud voice.

I am sorry, Swati.

Fine, so you have created this problem, handle it by yourself, bye, she said and hung up the call.

I love you Swati, I will do anything to get you in my life, I told her, but the call was already disconnected by her.

I was sobbing that night. I tossed and turned for the entire, night. I could not sleep. I burst out in tears at regular intervals. I thought Rohan can narrate false story to Abbay also, and he can create some scene with me if I stayed in my flat and there will be a lot more issues to deal with. I decided to visit a flat of my colleague very early in the morning the following day and spend some time there until the situation improves.

The next day, at a colleague's flat.

It was 8 PM the following day, and I was at my colleague's flat. I did not get any call from Swati that day, nor did she pick my call. I got upset and frustrated at the same time. After rambling too much in my head, I was unable to handle my emotions. My friend tried to cool me down, but I did not. I decided to call Ridhi and ask why did she share our photos with Rohan.

Hi Ridhi, Aarav here, I spoke on the phone call.

Hi Aarav.

Why did you share our Manali photos with Rohan? I asked you to delete that, I told her with a barely audible voice. I wanted to talk about it peacefully rather than creating a scene again. I had exhausted all my strength.

Why what happened Aarav? She wanted to know.

Rohan shared all the photos to Swati's brother Abbay and her family got to know about me, now they have stopped her from talking and meeting to me, she will also be not there at the café even, my life got trashed Ridhi, I said.

I am sorry Aarav, Rohan forced me to send those photos, she told me.

But why Ridhi, you said you have deleted those photos, how can you share your best friend's private photos with anyone, I demanded answers from her.

I am sorry Aarav, I had no other options left, she said.

And why, can you please tell me, I wanted to know.

Rohan called me, and he was shouting at me, he said why did you go with Aarav on his bike to your home, Am I interested in you? Do I like you? He asked what I was doing at the medical store with you, I don't know why, but he behaved in such a terrible way, and who informed him about all this incident as I did not tell him anything about that day, she added.

It's Kreepesh who narrated a false story to him, and we got into a massive fight at the office, I informed.

He asked me to prove that I was not very close to you during the Manali trip and hence he asked for all the photos and I had to send it because I love him, I don't want to lose him, I never knew he would share it with Swati's brother, please forgive me Aarav, she said.

What if we get separated by this act, you know Ridhi that I have not done any wrong to you, and you also know I cannot stay without Swati, everything got over, I could not hold back my emotions.

I don't know what went wrong between you and Rohan, as I already had some doubt regarding Kreepesh manipulating behaviour, she told me.

What doubt? I asked.

Kreepesh often used to talk ill about you, but Rohan never did. Rohan never talked anything negative about you but Kreepesh was someone who always used to poke him regarding you, that's why I was hesitant to speak anything in front of Kreepesh that day, I don't know what relationship you had with Kreepesh, she said.

But why did Rohan not share his relationship he had with you with me for so long, I asked.

Actually, Rohan had decided to hide this from everyone, he never wanted anyone to compare their girlfriend with me in terms of anything, he loved me so much, it was our mutual decision, nothing else Aarav, she said.

Have I ever compared Swati with you? What would I have done if I had known that he is dating you? If I had known about Rohan that he was in a relationship with you, I would have never taken you to Manali with me, I said.

We were just friends during our Manali trip, She answered.

So why did he ask Manali photos if you were not dating him at that time, I asked.

I think he got pissed off only at the reason that you dropped me on your bike, he wanted to know if I ever got close to you or something, Rohan is not a bad guy Aarav, someone for sure has played a massive role in this, she said.

I was angry, I was sad, I decided I am not having any further discussions with her. All of them had some role in sabotaging my beautiful relationship I had with Swati.

Alright, bye, I disconnected the call without having any further conversation with her.

I did not eat anything that day. Even a glass of water was difficult to gulp down my throat. I was both afraid and anxious about Swati. For the first time, I was hit with a panic attack that night.

It was all Kreepesh who tried his level best to smother all my happiness and I decided to watch that M**dh*rc*od screaming in pain and begging for relief.

32

M**dh*rc*od Kreepesh, get out of your room, I reached Kreepesh flat and banged the door of his room with all the power that I had.

Nikal M**dh*rc*od, I smacked the door again.

I felt someone striding towards the door. As soon as he popped open the door and I spotted that the motherfucker was in front of my eyes. I clutched his neck and dragged him up against the wall of his room.

What happened Aarav, he was terrified, and his body was quivering with fear.

Why did you narrate a false story to Rohan about me and Ridhi? I asked while grabbing his neck.

I don't know anything about this, he was acting as if he was innocent.

Why did you do this? I questioned him again in a stern voice.'

You are judging me wrong Aarav, I have not said anything.

I dragged him vengefully and made him sit on his bed.

Why did you do that? I raised the question again.

Maine kuch nahi kiya Aaarav, he responded and was shaking with fear.

M**dh*rc*od, why did you do that? I slapped him right on his face.

I don't know anything, Aarav. He struggled to defend himself. Meanwhile, I slapped him a few more times.

Just shut up M**dh*rc*od, I punched him this time.

I really don't know anything, what happened Aarav, he tried to open his mouth again.

M**dh*rc*od, was I buying condoms at the medical store, was I looking to sleep with Ridhi? This is what you said to Rohan, I asked strangulating his neck this time.

No Aarav. Please leave me. He was begging.

M**dh*rc*od, should I fuck you with the same condom which I bought, I smacked him.

Meanwhile, his roommate showed up from somewhere, and he decided to pull Kreepesh away from me. I pushed him away with my hands.

Hey, what happened, why are you abusing and lashing out at Kreepesh, his roommate wanted to know.

Get out of my matter, I shouted.

Hold on, what happened, he asked again.

Get out of my matter, you M**dh*rc*od, I abused his roommate.

Meanwhile, Kreepesh attempted to escape and run away from the room. I attacked him from behind and kicked him. He fell on the ground, I rushed over to him, I slapped him again. I punched him a few times on his face. I reached for his neck and tried to strangulate him. I would have strangulated that M**dh*rc*od to death that day. He was crying out for help. He was unable to breathe and could have fainted anytime. Seeing that, his roommate roped in some of the other guys from other rooms, and they did their best to protect Kreepesh.

Koi beech mei nahi ayega M**dh*rc*od, I lashed out and abused all of them.

Two of them among those four guys marched towards me and grabbed me from behind and signalled Kreepesh to move away from the room quickly. That M**dh*rc*od

Kreepesh escaped. The other two guys started kicking me on my stomach. I crumbled in pain. I decided to defend myself, but they were four of them, and I was the only one. I was convinced that silent manipulator Kreepesh had successfully teamed up these guys? If these guys had known what kind of guy that Kreepesh is, they would have never helped him escape from me. "M**dh*rc*od, akele lad, if you are a child of a single father, I abused all four of them. One of the guys punched me on my face and I started bleeding from my mouth. I still kept hitting them back with whatever energy I had. My heartbeat started beating faster. They punched my face and nose again, they kicked my abdomen area, they smacked on my chest. I was unable to defend myself more until the owner of the flat arrived.

What the hell is happening here, the owner yelled in a very loud voice. She was probably a 40-year-old lady.

All of them who were holding me got scared and left me instantly. I flopped on the floor while I was still bleeding from my mouth.

Why is he bleeding, the owner asked.

None of the guys spoke anything, and they got huddled around each other.

Who is he, and Why is he bleeding, and why were you all fighting? She spoke again.

He came to have a fight with Kreepesh, we were protecting Kreepesh, one of those guys said.

Where is Krepeesh, she wanted to know.

He ran away, one of the guys told her.

You get out of my flat at once, go back to where you have come, or otherwise I will file a police complaint against you, she sternly warned me.

Call Kreepesh and you all of them call your parents right away or else I will call in police, she also threatened all those four guys.

I got up while writhing in pain to move out of the room.

You all four of you get out of my flat in the morning tomorrow along with Kreepesh, I would rather not tolerate this kind of disturbance in my flat, pack your bags and leave tomorrow, or I will throw you at the police station, she shouted at them again, this time with a lot more anger in her voice.

I made my way out of the flat laboriously, as I was in a lot of pain.

M**dh*rc*od Kreepesh you got saved today, I will make sure next time, I meet you, I shall strangulate you to death. I abused him while leaving his flat.

I rushed back to my flat full of enmity. However, my mouth was still bleeding. I applied some medications and collapsed on the bed. My colleague was not present that time. I was all alone. I did not have any idea how things turned so much in a couple of days. I was worried. I raised my hands to my head and broke out. I could not stay away from Swati, I said to myself. All of them have conspired against me. I did not receive any call from Swati that day and that broke me from inside. I picked up my bike, and decided to get back to my flat because I was not comfortable having heavy emotions at my colleague's flat. I should allow myself to let my emotions flow. I was cursing myself for fighting with Rohan. I wanted to listen to Swati's voice, but she was not picking up my call. I did not consume anything that day, I panicked all night from the pain I was suffering.

33

"Papa is planning to get me married Aarav" Swati informed me while tearing up on the phone call.

Why? What happened, Swati? Is everything alright? Why this sudden decision? I asked her, and I was sweating with my nervousness.

I don't have any idea Aarav, papa was angry that day when he saw our pictures and came to know about all these things, and today I have heard him discussing with mummy to find a groom for me. He even phoned many of the relatives to find someone for me so that he can get me married anytime soon:I am afraid, Aarav. You know that I can't live without you, please do something, she continued while elucidating the matter and was incessantly shedding tears.

Swati, please don't cry; I will find some way, but they have to ask for your consent while getting you married, how can they do it on their own, I asked, and I was indignant.

My father is very conservative regarding love marriage, none of the family members have ever had a love marriage before, someone in my relation did it years ago and she died, she spoke, and went unresponsive.

Her words tore my heart into a million pieces, I went absolutely motionless for a few seconds. I was certain that my family was the one who did not believe in love marriages, but it was Swati's family too. She never ever told me that her father is very conservative. For the first time in my life, I was unable to decide what to speak and how to act in that situation. I was struggling to hear her break down in a way that she was doing. After cramming too many negative thoughts inside my head, I regained my inner strength and I began to speak again.

But Swati I am a software engineer, well-settled, and I earn good, why can't your parents accept me, I told her.

My father will not understand this Aarav because he won't allow a love marriage and he also

saw our pictures together, she said again.

Swati you must know this, I can't live without you, I will die if I don't see you around me, I will pull you out of your house and marry you in the court if everyone is against us, that's all I can say, but I won't leave you a day without me, I responded in a strong voice.

No Aarav, I cannot do a court marriage, please understand, she told me.

Why can't you do that, don't you love me Swati, I argued with her and was resentful.

I can't go against my parents in this way Aarav, what would they think about me, she added.

If they really love you, why don't they ask your consent for marriage, what kind of love is this, I sought answers from her.

Aarav, they were having discussions about my marriage, they are not getting me married even without asking me, there is still time Aarav, she said.

I don't know what do you want me to do then, you want to leave me for your parents' happiness, am I right Swati, I responded to her.

Aarav, I want you to reach out to both my family and your family and convince them, and get married, and not in a court, I want the whole family to be happy, she added.

So what if everyone is not happy about getting us married, will you still be their source of happiness, and will you leave me then, I wanted to know.

I can't go against my father, that's it, she said on the call.

Why can't you go, I raised my voice and shouted at her.

You know why my brother and I look after the café and my father stays at home, do you know the real reason, she added on the call.

How would I know the reason if you don't tell me the real truth, I was frustrated.

My father got seriously ill few years back in 2017 and was later diagnosed with Type 2 Diabetes and because of that one of his kidneys got extremely damaged, and he also suffered a minor Heart Attack, and we decided that my brother and I will look after the café since then, do you want me to do a court marriage with you and go against my father who is already suffering from illness, what if he cannot handle this situation well and something happens to him after that, Will I be able to forgive myself then, tell me what do you think now, she asked.

I was motionless and I had nothing to say. I was repressing my emotions. I did not wish to break down in front of her, who was already stressed out.

Please convince both the families Aarav if you want me to get married to you, this is the only option left, I know you are a good guy and my parents will accept you if they get to know you personally and not judge you with those pictures of us and so does your family, she advised.

I did not let out a single word.

I am going now Aarav, I will call you in some time, she told me and cut off the call.

I rested on my bed, and I was deeply disturbed after having a phone call with Swati. It killed me from inside and I felt like the whole world had stopped in front of my eyes, my life was like a deciduous tree which was loosing its leaves, and I knew that there was no chance of survival. I also knew how tough it was to convince my family back home for a love marriage, and now she informed me that her father is a non-believer of love marriage, which she never spoke of it before. She never reported that her father had an illness and that's why he chose to remain at home more often, and she couldn't go against her ill father to marry me. I permitted my suppressed emotions to erupt in full force. I could not hold back my tears. Fuck you my destiny, you motherfucker, I abused my destiny. I can't even convince my parents back home for a love marriage, and then I have to convince her parents too, what should I do now? I shouted and asked myself. She is not even ready to get married in a court. The only option left for me is to convince both the families and get married, and I have to do this all alone.

I had never expected that one terrible fight would result in so much trouble in my life. I knew it was going to be difficult to marry Swati, but the situation would have been different if I had been given a few more years to convince my family and her family and if those pictures would have not been forwarded by Rohan, her father would not have wanted her to get married so soon and would not have such a bad impression of mine in his head. All the events went against me and my relationship with Swati. Everything seemed to happen all of a sudden and my life was shattered completely. Both Rohan and Kreepesh ruined my life with the help of Ridhi, whom I trusted so much. They took away all my happiness from me, my mental health got worse than ever.

In the next few days, I could feel Swati in front of my eyes in flashes, I badly missed our best moments together. I barely had few calls in the entire day. Am I such a bad person? I asked myself. My life got torn apart so quickly, everything was going well for me, but this turn of events completely ripped my soul into smithereens.

I did not have any idea what to do next, what to say, how to act, all that I knew was if I lose Swati, I will lose myself.

34

After few weeks....
How much is the bill, I asked the cashier.
Rs 3000 sir, he responded.
Do you also need carry bags, sir?, he asked.
Please, I responded.

I cleared the amount by swiping my card in a wine shop inside a mall and took home a few bottles of wine, vodka, beer, and whiskeys. They had become my best friends for sometime after getting massacred by my very own friends whom I venerated so much. Smoking and drinking ended up being my daily habit.

Days soon expanded into weeks, and I completely stopped going to my office. I did not even attend a single day of my office after I was suspended. I would rather not see the faces of the two most vicious motherfuckers, Rohan and Kreepesh, in the office. I was battling to stabilize my emotions. I merely had any calls with Swati. The worst part was that I had been forced to drink and smoke to cope with the worst feelings I was going through in my life ever. I avoided talking to anyone on phone calls or even socializing with people outside. The entire day I used to lie on my bed and do nothing apart from being surrounded by empty bottles of whiskey, vodka, wine, and full packets of cigarettes.

The delightful memories that I had with Swati shared together flooded my mind. It had turned into weeks since I last met her. I remembered the way her enchanting eyes would sparkle when she smiled and the way her hair used to fell in loose waves down her back and she would share a lovely expression. Her voice was more than music to my ears. My eyes ached when I played back all the beautiful memories that I had with her.

Drinking and smoking became my usual habit. It was my escape and my way of dealing with my pain. Whenever I would feel worse, all that I would say to myself was that 'I am Fine' and all that I needed was a pack of cigarettes and wine.

Soon, I was trapped in a whole new world of depression and addiction, and I didn't know how to escape that beautiful world of addiction that was helping me counter my never-ending pain.

It was near to a month and I merely had a few calls in a week with Swati. I had given up going to the office permanently after I was suspended. I used to remain in my room the entire day, and I was in serious depression. I was addicted to alcohol and smoking. I had abandoned taking calls from anyone. I did not speak well even with my family members and that worried them. They felt perhaps something was wrong with me. I was still waiting for Swati to give me all the information that was happening at her home. She used to call me a few times in a week and talk for a few minutes, only to convey me that I was going to lose her and I had to do something very soon. Her Father had got too serious about getting her married soon, accompanied by her mother. I was still unsure what I should do next. Being locked in my flat for the entire day made me as lonely as ever. I got ill. I gazed into my mirror and I could not recognize myself for a second. I had a long messy hair, hollowed cheeks, red eyes, dark spots had developed under my eyes, my beard was unshaved. I never knew I would look such ugly someday.

Beauty has no real value when there is no peace.

I started off consuming 2 bottles of wine in a single day, and smoking cigarettes was countless. I used to vomit frequently. Instead of having healthy food, I was willing to be dependent on unlimited smoking and drinking. I didn't know how many countless bottles of wine and whiskeys were kept on the table in my room and beneath my bed.

I was dying to meet Swati, but I could not. I did not know what would happen next in my life, and when. I believed my destiny was cursed. Nicotine was my best friend, and I liked inhaling smoke through my veins. My room was full of smoke all around that surrounded me like warriors who helped me to wrestle with my endless pain. I gulped down a peg of wine and that rushed through my throat and satisfied my hunger. When I used to be in hangover, I would hardly remember anything, but when I would come back to my senses. I would start recalling all the memories of me and Swati having a conversation at the café, flirting with each other. I could see her smiling and laughing. I wanted to hear Tripathi ji from her sweet voice, but all I could hear was "Please do something Aarav".

I received so many calls from my colleagues and my Manager to report to the office without any delay or else I will be terminated, but I did not answer any call whatsoever. I had no strength left to sit and work in my office with all the pain that I was enduring. I only wished to have Swati in my life, and by each passing day it felt like I was going far away from her. I wanted to meet her desperately, but I could not.

I intended to call her several times, but she was not picking up my calls. I suspected that her family members were keeping constant eyes on her so that she couldn't connect with me in any way. I was in such a Soul-destroying pain. I wanted to fade away for some time and never return to this cruel world again.

35

"Swati, please help me, don't break off the call", I was beseeching her to talk to me. I felt like I was very lucky that day as she quickly picked up my call.

What happened?, she answered in a minimally plaintive voice.

I want you to meet me Swati or else I will not be alive any more, I told her and I could not hold back my emotions.

I can't Aarav, you already know that my family members are so mad at you, how can I meet you, she responded. Alright, I am going now, she added.

No, Please, Don't you love me any more Swati, I interrupted her, and I was struggling to speak further with all the locked-up emotions that I had.

Hmmm, she gave an answer.

Tell me that you don't love me any more, and I will kill myself, I warned.

I love you Aarav, but I am not well, please understand, she said.

Please meet me for once Swati, only for 10 minutes, I want to see you, I can't live without you any more.

What if you have to live without me? She responded.

I can't, and I never will, I will prefer dying if I don't see you around me, I cried and my heart was smashed into torn pieces.

Everyone says that, but people move on easily and that's the truth, she told me.

How can you say this to me, Swati, you know that I love you, have you already decided that you would leave me for your family, I questioned, and my tone was barely audible.

Did I tell you that I have decided anything, why don't you understand Aarav, you have to convince my family and your family to marry me, and you are not doing anything, you are just sitting at your flat imagining some miracle will happen, and we will get married, things are getting out of hand Aarav, please think about that.

So you think that I'm sitting idle at my flat doing nothing, don't I love you Swati, I don't want to lose you, I have stopped eating entirely, I have lost a lot of weight, my life is worse than hell without you, I have decided to go to my home and convince my family, but please meet me for once, I want to see you around me, I was begging her to meet me somewhere.

When are you heading to your home then, she questioned.

I will leave soon, Swati, I told her.

When, she inquired again.

Soon, I added.

You are still deciding Aarav, I don't think you want to marry me, she said in a stern voice.

I love you, Swati.

You will convince your family after I get married to someone else, right, she seemed extremely frustrated on the call.

I need some more time, I am planning how to convince my family and your family, I replied.

Still planning? So why did you create this problem now if you still require time to talk to your family, she added.

I did not do it intentionally Swati, I never knew Kreepesh would play such a wicked game with me, I told her, and I was getting very emotional with her every word spoken and the harsh way she was talking to me.

Swati, please don't talk to me like this, I burst out in tears after trying to suppress my emotions for a very long time on the call.

Please meet me once Swati, I requsted with all the heavy emotions in my voice.

I can't Aarav, please understand, if my brother finds out, then you know what he can do, things will get worse.

If you don't meet me, I am probably dead, what's more worst than that Swati, I said.

Don't use words like this, I love you Aarav, I am myself dying to see you, I wish I could feel you close to me, she burst out in tears this time.

Please do something Swati, I know you can do it, please meet me once, I pleaded.

Aarav, but, she hesitated.

Please, Swati if you wish to see me alive, I said.

Okay, I will sneak out of my home at 1 AM in the midnight when everyone would be sleeping, you meet me at our nearby park that is close to my house. She had a plan.

Today?, I asked.

Not today, this Sunday, my brother won't be there at home, I will somehow manage maa and papa, she told me.

Okay, you will come na, I asked.

I will, Aarav.

Please wear a mask, I don't want anybody to recognize you, she added.

Okay.

She put off the call.

I was a tiny bit happy that day, and also at ease that Swati listened to me. I got enough courage to head back to my home and convince my family, and then I would win over her family and marry her. But I was also not sure whether my parents would stand with me, I would have married her in the court because I could not live without her, but she cannot go against her ill father, I had no other options left whatsoever.

This was the most expensive bet of my life, either I would win Swati or lose her.

If I win her, I shall be the happiest person on the earth, and If I lose her, I would lose myself forever, and I would be left with nothing, but I would never allow her to lose her happiness.

I had a plan that was solely for her happiness.

After 5 Days ....

Sunday....

It was closer to 12 AM in the midnight and Swati confirmed with me on the call that she would be right there at the nearby park of her house.

I headed towards my drawer in my room and took out a small wooden box that I bought a few days before, and I was going to give that wooden box to Swati.

It took me a lot of pain and suffering and an abundance of tears to create this wooden box for Swati that I would give it to her.

All that I wanted was that she would stay happy no matter what. I did not know what was coming next for me, whether I would get Swati in my life or not, whether I would be even alive or not, I did not know anything. Whether I would lose Swati or I will be dead, I still desire to see her smiling even when I am looking at her from the hell's door.

I hid the wooden box inside my jeans pocket and made my way straight to the ground floor, where my bike was parked. I headed to my bike and accelerated it full of mixed feelings in my head and heavy eyes and raced to the park that was close to her house.

It was around 12:30 AM in the midnight and I finally got to the park at Sector 47, which was close to her house, and I sat on a cemented chair that was available in the park where people used to sit more often during the evening. I sat and began waiting for Swati. After 15 minutes of complete silence, I shifted my eyes, and I saw her approaching closer. I turned happy, and I stood up almost immediately. I was still wearing a helmet so that no one can recognize me in that dark night. I was so delighted to see her walking towards me after a very long time. I could not stop my eyes to share tears of joy.

She strolled closer, and I sprinted towards her and took off my helmet.

Aarav. She identified me and removed her mask.

I clutched her hands to feel her presence, I could not believe whether she was standing in front of me for real or was it a dream, I got completely lost for a few seconds.

As soon as I opened my eyes, I saw Swati stroking me hair.

What have you done Aarav, have you lost a lot of weight, she asked, and she seemed concerned.

Swati, I have lost 7 kg of weight, I informed her about my poor health.

Why are you not eating anything, she gently stroked my cheeks.

I have always felt that I was very brave, in fact, braver than everyone else around me, but I literally broke out in tears seeing her in front of my eyes and I knew it could be even one last time that I was meeting her, I could not cope with my emotions. She tried her best to settle me down, but I was struggling to hold back my tears. I never imagined I would become so weak someday.

Aarav, please don't cry, what happened, tell me. She spoke, wiping my tears with her fingers.

I can't live without you Swati, you don't pick up my calls, you don't talk to me any more.

You know na Aarav, if my family members would spot me talking to you, they will rush to your flat and I don't want that to happen, I love you.

Why did you call me Aarav, is there something you want to share, she gently touched my ears.

I am heading back to my home tomorrow itself to convince my family, and then I will win over your family. I have no other options left, If I have to stay alive, you have to be there with me throughout my life. I said with my reddened eye.

But Aarav. She was trying to tell something.

I gazed at her.

What if you can't Aarav, she added.

I will, Swati, I assured her in a very fainted voice.

Swati I have something for you, I want to gift you something before I head back to my home, I told her.

What Aarav? She was confused.

I pulled out the wooden box from my pocket and handed it to her.

What that's Aarav. She was puzzled.

It's a wooden box that contains my love for you, but please don't open it. I requested.

Ohh So why are you giving me this wooden box, if I should not open it, are you alright Aarav, she was concerned by my bizarre behaviour.

You can only open this wooden box when you are extremely worried in your life and could not decide what to do next, this box will have all the answers to your problems, I told her.

Aarav, I think you are not alright, why would I be worried, what problems will I have? Are you not coming back to me, why should I wait to open this box, and what have you put inside that box, she inquired.

Please, Swati. Take my swear, that you won't open it, please open it only when I am not around you, I requested again.

But you are going to convince everyone na, so you will always be around me, so this wooden box does not make any sense, she pointed out.

Swati don't argue, this box has all my love for you, and I want you to open it before your wedding, I said.

But I want to marry you, Aarav, she said, and was confused.

Yes Swati, we will get married but open this box before your wedding and not when I am around you, Open it when you are alone, I said.

I don't know what to say and what do you want to say, as you wish Aarav, but please go and check up your health, I don't think you are alright, are you depressed, I can't see you like this, she lightly stroked my cheeks.

I love you Swati, I kissed her forehead.

Will you come back na Aarav, I love you Aarav, I can't live without you, she said with her teary eyes.

If I don't come back, consider me dead, Swati, I told her.

I could see tears pouring out of her eyes.

Swati, please take care of yourself, I will be back soon, and we will be happy thereafter, pray for me, I assured her.

I love you Aarav.

I asked her to hurry back to her house as it was late midnight. She turned and moved towards her house and looked at me back. I waved my hands. With each moving steps of her, I could see her fading and going away from me.

With all the heavy emotions, I walked back to my bike and decided to leave for my flat.

36

March 2021, Patna

I never enjoyed playing chess. In fact, this game was the only one that never excited me, but I never knew I would be forced to play chess for the first time in my real fucking life and I had no prior experience to that. I had to play and win Swati. Every move I make would be decisive for me and If I initiated a bad move, it was guaranteed that I would lose Swati. This was the most costly task I would have ever done in my life. The time had finally sprung up that I was afraid of, and that swept away my sleep. I was scheduled to convince my traditional conservative Brahmin family, who holds belief in arrange marriage of same caste, to marry a non-Brahmin and then I had to go back to win over the conservative family of Swati. I remembered the famous proverb that I used to facetiously share with my friends when I was a teenager, 'na ghar ka na ghaat ka'. I was in a very similar situation. I had to play and win this game and marry her anyhow. I did not know the outcome of this, all that I knew was that, if I lose to my family, I would lose Swati and I would not even get a chance to convince Swati's family. If I win to convince my family, I would atleast get a chance to convince Swati's family, and I would still have a chance to marry her. If I lose Swati by any means, I will lose myself, if I lose myself, I will have nothing left with me and I shall be a body without a soul …

It was a Monday night at around 9 PM, and I was travelling back to my home with the hope that I would marry Swati. I prayed God to be kind to me and my destiny to forgive me if I have ever made a mistake. I had lost my appetite and I had not consumed any food what's so ever in the last few days. I only had some energy drinks to keep my body moving since it was burdened with a lot of pain. It was probably around 9:30 PM, and I was about to leave for the railway station. My ticket was booked in 12274 HWH DURONTO EXP and its scheduled arrival time was at 12:40 AM at New Delhi railway station and I would reach Patna in around 12 hours.

I booked the cab online and started waiting anxiously as there was still half an hour left for the cab to arrive as shown in the App. With stinging red moist eyes and an explosion of emotions, I locked my room and carried my trolley and bag out.

I had a conversation and asked the cab driver to get me on board from the nearby chowk which was 500'metres away from my flat and I decided to have a Walk to the chowk. I stepped out of my flat and began strolling with my trolley bag. As I was walking around, nothing appeared to feel good. Everything seemed so dull, I did not like the ambiance, I abhorred all the people passing by me. Anyway, I spent so many years in Delhi, but that day did not seem pleasant. I didn't quite understand what my destiny was trying to speak, but I felt so uneasy heading to the chowk. I was taking very shorter steps than usual. In Hindi, we say 'Begana'. The whole thing seemed to be begana for me that day.

I stepped into the cab and after an hour of non-stop battling with my emotions, overthinking, and replaying all the memories I had with Swati, I reached the New Delhi railway station. When the mind is idle, it starts to overthink more and more. I headed to the railway station and entered the waiting hall to wait for the train to arrive. It was close to 11:30 PM and there was still an hour for the train to arrive. I opted not to have any food as my lost appetite did not allow me.

I boarded the train and took my side lower birth. I had booked side lower birth intentionally since I knew this has to be one of the longest and toughest nights I would ever have in my life, and I was not planning to sleep even for a minute. Either I would win Swati or I would lose her, or I would lose both Swati and myself, I thought to myself. I was always a funny guy, but there was no smile on my face for weeks. I looked ugly, I lost weight, I had no facial expression, no interest, nothing. I absolutely did not know the strategy to manipulate someone to get my work done, I had always been a fun-loving straightforward guy. I never learned how to convince people by playing around with my words or something similar. I never thought I would be in such a troubling situation someday. I had no clue how I would convince my conservative parents and then Swati's parents. The more I thought, the more daunting a task it seemed to me.

I could not fall asleep even for a minute during my journey, I tried to ring Swati, but she did not pick up my call and the reasons were unknown. I took my phone and browsed her pictures in my gallery for the entire night. Her memories and photographs were a gift that somehow managed to plant a smile on my face for a few seconds. I snapped back all the wonderful memories that we had shared together.

After 12 hours of an over-emotional train journey, I finally reached Patna railway station. I hired a bike and headed to my home within half an hour. I thought I would rather not make a scene and talk anything to anyone during the daytime; hence, I decided that I would talk to my parents and family the next day. My mother could not even recognize me after seeing me, I had lost a lot of weight.

It was probably around 9 AM the next day. Everyone had their breakfast and the expensive game was about to start. I, along with my parents and my grandparents, were all present in the main hall. My grandparents were relaxing on the sofa, my father was standing right there in front of me, and to my right was my mother staring at me.

After a few minutes, ...

You will marry a baniya, you bastard, how dare you? My father lashed out at me and raised his voice in a way that I had never seen before in my life.

Don't you think about the values of the family Aarav, we are a Brahmin family, and you can only get married to a Brahmin. How can you even dream of marrying someone of another caste, maa added.

I was numb, my hands and feet were trembling, I was not answering but only listening to all the people around me.

What will the people say, have you ever thought anything about that? How would we walk out of our home and reveal our face to others? My grandfather said.

But I love her papa, I cannot live without her, I gathered some strength and said in a barely audible voice.

So what, don't you love your family any more, papa yelled.

I do papa, but I can't live without her.

You love a baniya, I have made my decision, I would not allow you to marry someone of another caste, only a Brahmin girl can be married and not a baniya, get that in your head, he said very bluntly.

I was losing Swati now and my raw emotions and all the memories that I had with her took over, my love for Swati compelled me to answer, and I decided to confront ...

Why can't we marry a baniya papa, our caste is not decided by birth, but it's our deeds that define our caste, it's written in Bhagwad Geeta, why can't I marry her, I love her and I will stay happy with her. What do you want, my happiness or your happiness? I confronted my father.

Don't you argue with me, Aarav, I will slap you, you are trying to sell our family's respect that we have built up over years? I have already said you can't get married to her, you can only get married to a Brahmin girl and that's final …

Please understand Aarav, it can't be done, Please be quiet, we are not supposed to marry a non-Brahmin, you can't marry her? maa tried to calm me down.

Why can't I marry a baniya? I cried with all the energy I had.

You can't, and you will not, papa shouted.

Why can't I? In fact, the entire world is a baniya. Isn't it, mom? When parents send their kids for higher education, they expect them to return everything with a high package placement and earning, isn't this something that a baniya does, isn't it a business, are we not a baniya then, I kept my point.

When we give someone money, we ask for it back, it's it what a baniya does? When we offer help to someone, we expect it back, it is not what a baniya does, a businessman does, I added.

You are sacrificing my happiness for your happiness, what should I call it now, isn't it not a profit setting that mainly involves business, I defended myself.

The entire world is a baniya dad, why can't I marry Swati? I love her and I will marry her …

You can't go against your family? My father shouted, and my mother rushed to him to deter him from slapping me.

Alright, papa, so you decide, which is more painful for you, your life without me? Or your life with Swati, I asked my father.

Everyone went numb, I never had such arguments in my family ever before.

My life without you all, Aarav. I would rather choose to die than see my son selling my hard-earned prestige in the society and throwing the family dignity into a mud, it's your decision now. Decide whether you want your life with the girl or your life without me. In fact, everyone who is standing here, life without me, he declared and left towards his room.

I lost the game, I lost the bet and I lost my beautiful caring and loving girlfriend Swati …

I began to shiver, my hands and feet all went wet. I was not blinking, tears rolled down my eyes. I was similar to a statue that could not move its feet. My emotions were looming over me. All that I can remember was that everyone left the main hall one by one, and I was still there begging my destiny to show some mercy and help me somehow.

I lost my girlfriend, I lost my Swati whom I loved so much. My love was strangulated to death. I knew that there would be no Aarav any more.

I got down on my knees and invited my destiny to punish me. I closed my eyes, but I could feel Swati was still there, in my eyes hovering around waiting for my return and I felt like she was asking' Are you coming back na Aarav?

37

March 2021, Kolkata

I am looking for a one BHK flat, I expressed to the broker while I was milling around the streets of salt lake, sector 5, in Kolkata.

I was a stranger to the city and had no clue as to where I should reside in Kolkata. I browsed for some information online, and I learned that Salt Lake might be the best place to stay, specially in Kolkata.

Rs 10000 to Rs 12000 will be the rental cost and my brokerage charge is extra, If you are okay, I will show you the flats.

Which particular place is this? I questioned the broker.

This is Nayapatty NP Block which comes under Salt Lake, sector 5, he responded.

Okay, I said in a barely audible voice.

He walked me around and showed me some vacant rental flats.

He showed me some 1BHK flats, and it was no good at all. It was mostly people's own homes, and they converted their ground floor or top floor of their living home to flats, while they themselves resided in one of those floors while the other floors were available to rent. I realized it was a good business. I did not like any of those flats. The rooms were not properly looked after, it seemed like so many people were staying in the same rooms to avoid rent cost. The washrooms were poorly maintained. I asked the same thing with the broker as why does these rooms look so filthy and not well cleaned. He replied," mostly people who reside in this area are private employees or students; hence they rent the flat and share rooms with their colleagues and flatmates as most of them are bachelors.

But these are not flats, but the homes of people, I was confused.

He responded,"People here allow renting their ground floor or other floors to make extra rental income while they themselves stay on one of those floors. This is a packed area because of so many engineering colleges and MNC's around. Plenty of students and employees chose this area to stay.

I inquired the broker about renting an apartment similar to what I had in Delhi, I was ready to pay any rent, but the rooms should be decent enough. Although I had left my job, but I had some savings to rent at least a good flat to stay. I could not stay in those dingy rooms.

Apartments are allowed only for married people and not bachelors, the broker told me.

Is it like that, why can't I get into an apartment, I was unsure.

He said no, you have to remain in these flats only, tell me quick, or otherwise these flats will also be booked by someone else, there are hardly any flats left In salt lake area because it's an IT hub and college area and most of the employees and students stay in this area, he repeated this again. I suspected he was trying hard to settle me into any flat and get his brokerage charge from me.

I was in no mood for further discussion, I asked him to show me some more flats. I would rather not stay in people's homes known as flats here, and they would catch me every day what I was doing inside my room. My life was already fucked up from before.

After stepping into 4-5 flats, which I did not like at all. He introduced me to a flat whose owner was a retired government teacher and his house was a 5-storey building and a room on the 3rd floor was vacant. I thought this might be the best flat for me as there were a lot of people who were staying in his house and I will go unnoticed every day. I asked the broker to show me the room.

It was a 1 BHK kind of flat where there was one small room with an attached bathroom, a dining area and a tiny kitchen space. The room was well painted and cleaned, and I decided to rent that flat.

Alright, the rent will be Rs, 10000 per month, and you have to pay 2 months of deposit and one month of brokerage fee, electricity bill will be extra, the broker stated.

Meanwhile, the owner arrived and began asking me a few questions.

What do you do? The owner inquired.

I work in a MNC uncle, I lied.

Which MNC, he asked.

L an T uncle, I lied again.

Do you have to go to office here, he asked.

Uncle its work from home currently, but I do have to commute to my office frequently and report there, I added.

Okay, Okay, he responded.

I assumed I was able to convince him anyhow, as he was not a very technical guy.

Pay RS, 20000, which is 2 months of rent to this ID, he popped out his phone and shared with me the UPI I'd and his Bank account to pay him online.

I instantly sent Rs, 20000 to his bank account.

Please pay my brokerage fee, which is one month of rent, Rs 10000, the broker interrupted.

I paid him Rs, 10000 immediately as I did not wish to see him any more. He looked like a lier and fraudster to me.

I bought in some new bedding, bedsheets and pillow from a nearby shop that day itself and I shifted into a new flat in a new place all alone away from everyone.

After a week...

I had no Intentions to join any job again, as I could not be able to do that. I did search for some Software engineering jobs in Kolkata, but I was not well, and I thought I will not be able to work any more. I decided not to join any job anytime soon.

It was almost two weeks of living in my new flat in Kolkata, and I slipped into depression. I was lonely, I had just nobody to talk to. I had frequent mood swings, I had stopped talking to anyone and picking up calls from my home. I was unable to socialize with people around. I was missing Swati, I wanted to talk to her.

That night was the longest night for me, I was so badly missing Swati, I was dying to see her, but soon I came back to my senses when I realized that I had failed to convince my parents to marry her. I remembered that I have blocked her social media accounts and her contact. I had also broken my SIM card before coming to Kolkata. I longed to revisit my phone gallery and see her pictures smiling, but I had deleted all of those photos before coming here. I purchased photo recovery tools and Apps to get those deleted photos back, but I could not recover any photos. I started breaking down, heavily, after remembering her. I craved to be hugged by her and rest in her arms. There was nobody around to support me during these though times. I had no mental support, I had no friends. I believed, she might be still eagerly waiting for me to return to her and marry her, but I was a coward who ran away from this situation to a new place and I left my love of my life, Swati behind. I did not know what she might be going through and what her parents had decided for her future. I got severe panic attacks that night, my feet were shaking, my body was sweating, all that I wished was to talk to her for once, but I couldn't. I was cursing myself for deleting all her memories from my phone.

I love you Swati, I cried so hard.

After one month in Kolkata....

It was almost 9 AM and I woke up to have my breakfast. I went into the kitchen where I had assembled a few bottles of wine, whiskey, vodka, and beer and pulled out the bottle of vodka and carried it back to my bed. I lounged on my bed and prepared the hookah which I had bought recently with a strong flavour, and I sorted my packets of cigarettes. I lighted the hookah, and had a shot of vodka, I used to smoke cigarettes with each shot I took of either vodka, wine, or whiskey. The lunch menu was the same for me, after having some sort of food which I could barely eat, I used to sit and drink. The dinner was similar. This is how I passed my time in Kolkata, away from everyone and not speaking to anyone. My family members assumed I had joined a new job in one of the top MNC in Kolkata. They thought I have moved on, but I was still immersed in my love, Swati. How could I forget her, it was impossible to forget her until I die.

This continued for several weeks and I fell into severe depression. I was struggling to forget Swati, and I was unable to do anything either. It surpassed two months in Kolkata and without having any sort of communication with Swati. The pain was getting worse day by day. My room was filled with wine, whiskey, and smoke of cigarettes all around. Beneath my bed, there were only bottles of wine and used packets of cigarettes scattered. I had lost a lot of weight. This went on.......

One day, I gradually starting thinking to harm myself because of my severe depression and I decided to get medical help. I was not that strong enough any more to visit a psychiatrist in the nearby locality and get myself treated. Although, I set out to visit a psychiatrist nearby, but I made it back to my room from the entrance itself after seeing so many ill patients at the clinic. I just could bear all this alone.

After finding, it was difficult to cope with my depression, I went ahead to take medical help online and get counselling. I looked over so many websites online and Apps and got stumped at "YOUR LIFE CARE" which was providing online counselling services and I could also connect with a psychiatrist. I was seeking some medication urgently. I placed an order with them to connect me with a psychiatrist that can guide me to control my mental health. I was even ready for online counselling. I could not speak about my pain with anyone, I was all alone and I required counselling or medical treatment urgently, or otherwise I would have not survived.

After placing an order, I soon found out that they were fraudsters, there was no one in their company who was providing counselling services, and they had listed fake profiles of psychiatrists, and they were making fun of people who were in depression and eating their money. It was all bad business. I felt horrible, I was hoping for some more websites' to connect but to my disappointment, all were just fake business and no one provided any real support. Some websites were very expensive, and they included just half an hour of counselling, My pain was too large to be shared in just half an hour, it could take days. I thought, I could have gone to a psychiatrist's clinic and got treated.

After a week....

Unable to wrestle with my depression, I gathered some strength and decided to visit a nearby clinic. I booked an appointment online with DR.Sambhavi Dey who was a psychiatrist and went to her clinic all alone to get my mental treatment done. To my pleasant surprise, the doctor was brilliant, and she heard everything whatever I said with full attention. I felt that she was somehow sad for me, as I was struggling with depression at a very young age.

She prescribed some medicines and shared me her personal number so that I can connect with her in case of an emergency. I was very satisfied with how she talked and behaved. But the worst part was that I never gave up drinking and smoking, which was denied by The doctor. I kept on drinking wine, vodka, whiskeys, beer, and smoking cigarettes every day. I was coughing so badly sometimes and vomiting after having an overdose of alcohol in my body. There were no popular brands of wine and vodka and whiskeys left, which were not introduced to my taste buds.

38

December 2021, Kolkata

After 6 months….
   Last week of December……
"I am going back to my room from my office maa, I lied to my mother on the phone call. My family members were convinced that I had joined a new job in L and T(MNC), and I have been working in that company since last 6 months. I have stayed here in Kolkata and have never headed to any other place during this time what's so ever. I was returning to my flat after having a cup of chai from a nearby Café and that reminded me of all the memories I had at Agarwal café and my love for Swati. I had still not moved on or forgotten her. She was still part of my life. I painfully missed her everyday. But I did not know what she might be feeling about me as I have left her since last 6 months and there has not been any single communication with her or any other people. I had no memories of her in my phone gallery, I desperately wanted to hear her voice, and she's calling me

'tripathi ji for one more time" but my destiny had turned completely blind. I had no idea what was happening in her life. Taking medications from a psychiatrist for my mental health had helped me to get out of severe depression to a certain extent, but I was still drinking and smoking a lot. I used to think about her at every moment of my life. I dumped her, but I constantly prayed for her happiness.

At 6:30 PM, Same day.....
After close to ten minutes, I entered my flat and I settled on my bed and gulped a glass of water. That day my gut feeling was making me nervous and the reasons were unknown. My instincts were trying to convey some message to me. I rubbed my eyes and could see Swati smiling. I tried my best to distract myself, but I could not. I was continuously and non-stop thinking about her. I felt as something wrong had happened for sure. After battling with my overthinking and missing Swati terribly, I pulled out my phone from my pocket and reinstated my Instagram Account, which I had deactivated 9 months ago when I blocked Swati from everywhere. I unblocked Swati on Instagram, but her profile was still private and there was no DP, I was not lucky enough to see her face, I therefore chose to unblock her brother Abhay and I did the same.

As soon as I unblocked her brother, I saw a post that was uploaded a day before. A post that chopped my love into a million pieces. A post that ripped my soul apart. A post that I would remember when I would be taking my last breath on my deathbed.

My love and my girlfriend, Swati was married to someone else......

The post was posted a day ago by her brother Abhay, and it was Swati's wedding day. The caption that her brother wrote was 'Happy married life, Swati'. I felt like I would die at that moment and my soul was begging to be taken away from my body, which was already dead from inside. I felt an enormous emotional pain, similar to a pain of needles piercing my entire body. I tried to stabilize myself, but I could not. I felt like someone was strangulating and killing me. The emotional pain was much more than the pain that people bear when they are about to die. Heavy Tears were streaming down my eyes, and I was smiling. I saw Swati with her cousins who were taking her for the varmala, and she looked absolutely stunning. I zoomed the post to see if Swati was smiling, but she was not. I tried to sneak a peek at her husband's photos, but it was not clearly visible and it was blurry. All the focus was on Swati. I attempted to check some more accounts to pick up some more photos, I got some photos from her cousins' account where they uploaded the pics of both the groom and bride. I came to know she was married in a Gupta Family. My tears were still dripping, but I never understood why I was smiling. Was it the immense emotional pain that I was going through? I had no answers for that. I guess I could not bear that immense pain and hence my mind was reacting differently. I had never imagined Swati would get married to someone else, even in my dream, but this was not a dream but a reality.

After sometime, I was struggling to control my emotions when I saw some other posts where Swati had worn wedding bangles in her hands and put on a mehndi that probably had her husband's name written on it. Something that I feared the most. The sindur on her forehead sliced my soul into a million pieces. I was already dead, and I would rather not survive either. I lost everything that I feared. It was around half an hour going through all the posts, and then it was the time to let me emotions flow.

She Was Only Mine

I sobbed like a small kid that day.

My hands started trembling, I could not hold my phone. I started sweating, I was continuously feeling that pain of needles piercing my entire body. It was not physical pain but an emotional pain which I witnessed for the first time in my life. I cried, I cried my soul out. I started having panic attacks. I locked my room from inside and I started shouting and screaming. I threw all the things that we're around me. I kicked all the items that were present in my room. After half an hour of going through immense emotional pain and crying heavily, I sat on my bed and gulped a glass of water. I tried to calm myself down, but I could not.

Fuck you destiny, M**dh*rc*od, *Fuck you* M**dh*rc*od................ *I CRIED*............

I loved Swati more than myself and "she was only mine ". Seeing her married to someone else was that kind of pain, which I would never like to bear. I would rather die than see her with someone else, but she was already married to someone else. I saw her posts so many times that Swati's pictures started reflecting in my eyes. I remembered all those moments when she cared and loved me. I recalled her caressing my cheeks with so much love.

I laid on my bed in an uncontrolled way. Then I calmed myself down and realized that it was my decision to get Swati married to someone else. Yes, it was me who wanted to get her married to someone where she would be happy and respected. If I had married her by any means, she would never get that respect in my family which she deserved. She was worthy of all the love in her life.

When I last met her in a nearby park to her house, I handed her a wooden box and I asked her not to open it. She can only open it when she feels she is unable to decide anything in her life. It had all the answers, as I had told her.

It took me enormous strength to create that secret box for her. I was sure she opened that box before she got married to someone else.

The wooden box that I gave her consisted of a blue colour bracelet and a letter which I wrote for her. I always wanted her to wear that bracelet on her wedding day. This was the same bracelet I bought for her in Varanasi. I scrolled back to Instagram and I rechecked the photos to see if she was wearing that bracelet on her wedding day. I zoomed the photos and happy tears started pouring down from my eyes when I saw my beautiful Swati had put on that bracelet in her right hand just below her wedding bangles.

The letter inside the Box :

Hi Swati ...

I am sorry, please forgive me if you can. I cannot marry you and I knew this always that I would be unable to marry you, still I chose to get you into a relationship that had no future. I dumped you. I used you for myself. I wasted three years of your precious life where you had your opportunity to date and marry someone of your choice, but I even took away that opportunity from you already knowing that I am not going to marry you. Someone who might love you would never run away from you, but I did. I don't know when you are reading this letter, and I guess your wedding is closer. There is no situation where you could lose in this world apart from your marriage. All that I can say is that I never convinced my family, the results were already known to me. I played with your emotions. All that I can ask is, please marry to someone who deserves you truly and someone who would love you from the bottom of their heart and not like me. You deserve a family where you would be loved, pampered and respected. I bought a beautiful bracelet for you in Varanasi and I want you to wear it on your wedding day. I don't know where I would be when you would get married, but I will find out your wedding pics and videos. I want you to wear that bracelet if you are happy with your wedding partner. I could not see you staying in an unhappy marriage after destroying your life. I never loved you, but if you have ever loved me, please wear the bracelet and convey me that you are happy with your partner and allow me to die peacefully.

I wish for your happiness.

Bye.....

I knew Swati loved me a lot. You cannot forget someone and their memories if you have no reasons to hate that person. I wrote this letter because I wanted Swati to hate me and curse me from the bottom of her heart so that she can move on easily and stay happy in her married life.....

39

After a week....

"Aarav, see this is my dining room 'she gripped my wrist and took me inside her house. She showed me her bedroom, her kitchen, her main hall and the balcony. It was a 3 BHK, flat. She requested me to rest on the sofa in her main hall and served some snacks and a glass of water. I am happy Aarav, this is my new home, she told me, looking into my eyes.

She rushed to her kitchen to bring my favourite adrak chai and suddenly, my phone rang, and it was "Swati Gupta" calling that popped up on my phone screen. I woke up and I was blown away. I opened my eyes and I realized that I was dreaming. Swati was married now, and she was Swati Gupta and not Swati Agarwal. I was struggling to breathe, I broke down, she appeared in my dreams only to communicate that she was happy. I didn't know what kind of dream that was, but that killed me from inside. I was always afraid of losing Swati, but I have lost her now.

I threw my phone out of frustration and got up to get a glass of water. I tried to soothe myself down, but I was unable to. I was trying to recall the dream which I saw where Swati held my hands and showed me her entire house. I could not believe what had just happened to me. Alright, I comforted myself, believing that she might be happy, and she wanted to tell this to me, but she could not and hence she showed up in my dream. I was concerned about her in-law's behaviour and nature and how would they take care of my love Swati and all the other people in her new house, but to some extent I was relieved that she was smiling wherever she was.....

I felt so lonely without her. I was dying to hear her voice for one last time, her beautiful lips speaking in front of me while exposing her adorable expressions, but I knew this will never ever happen again in my life. She was only mine, but she was not mine. I can only forever cherish the memories that we shared together. I didn't know whether she still loves me or hates me for what I have done to her, but I still love her and I will pray for her happiness and well-being wherever she is in her life.

I promise you Swati, I will love you until my last breath, you will always be mine, I will cherish all the beautiful memories we had together for my lifetime and I will respect your privacy and all the private moments we shared together. I will always worship your love that you had for me.

Happy Married life my love and stay blessed, I prayed for her happiness.........

If you truly love someone, what would you prefer to choose?
Your happiness or her happiness ?
If you choose your happiness, does it mean that you own your partner and can even destroy her happiness for your happiness if destiny does not favour your relationship ?
If you decide to choose her happiness, how would you feel if you find her in a happy loving relationship, but her partner is not you but someone else ?
Let me know your thoughts in the reviews......

It takes months and even years of hard work to write a novel. If you liked the story, all that I request you to please leave your review from whichever online platform you have bought this book from........
Wishing you lots of happiness in your life........

Author

Abhinav Ojha is a Computer Scientist, Indian Entrepreneur, cybersecurity expert and best-selling author of Engineering Textbooks. He is known as 'The Real Professor' of engineering textbooks. His best-selling book on ethical hacking and cybersecurity is used as a textbook in top 25 Engineering Institutes in India. Abhinav Ojha is widely known for his app marketing skills.

Abhinav Ojha is India's best and most selling ethical hacking and cybersecurity book author.

"She Was Only Mine" is his debut romance novel which is based on a true love story.

Abhinav has authored eight books as of now and has received several national and international awards for his achievements.

Some of his awards includes 'Young Entrepreneur Award' by Indian Achiever's forum, Young Achiever's award by Indian Achiever's forum, International Achiever's award for young author and others.

Abhinav Ojha is a passionate individual who loves technology more than anything else. He loves to explore new technical domains and spread his knowledge online or offline to others, either in the form of his writing or speaking.

Follow on Instagram : @abhinavojhaofficial